The Muse of Violence

Also by Bruce Hartman:

Perfectly Healthy Man Drops Dead

The Rules of Dreaming

The Muse of

Violence

a novel by

Bruce Hartman

Swallow Tail Press

Published by Swallow Tail Press,

Philadelphia, PA, USA

swallowtailpress.com

ISBN-10: 0-9889181-1-0

ISBN-13: 978-0-9889181-1-5

Cover design by Kit Foster

The Muse of Violence

The writers' group is just a memory now. I can still picture them sitting in my apartment—four women and two men in addition to myself—reading stories to each other in a search for fictional truth that seemed more important than real life. That was before death pulled up a chair and started spinning tales of its own. We were so naive, all we did was complain about the heat.

Now it's left to me to tell the story, flashing back to that brutal summer where the story begins and ends. The hottest summer in New York in ten thousand years, they called it. Maybe you'll believe my tale—if not, I can't blame you. But trust me when I say I'm not the only unreliable narrator you'll meet on this trip.

"The story begins," I told Eleanor, "when the conflict begins. Not one sentence before that." Eleanor fixed her eyes on the page in front of her, pursing her lips as she considered her response. I had spoken in my gentlest voice, and I hoped it was gentle enough. She was a kindly woman in her mid-fifties, a transplanted Midwesterner like myself, warm and well-meaning but always a little on edge. Critiquing her writing was a little like pointing out the flaws in your Mom's apple pie.

A financial consultant's wife, Eleanor had devoted herself to charity work and started writing after her children left the nest. Hers was a world of club luncheons and fund raising galas and wedding announcements in the *New York Times*, and I'm sure she faced the challenges of that world with quiet self-confidence. But as a writer she had to be humored like a child. She was so hesitant, so unsure of herself, that you had to admire her just for being there, baring her soul to a group of younger writers with the quick wits and quicker tongues of their generation. That night it was her turn to read, and she had begun her usual meditation on the frustrations of post-menopausal life on the East Side of Manhattan. A character named Margaret brooded in silence while her husband cheated on her and her grown children ignored her. There was emotion, but it was too bottled up to translate into drama. Hence my well-worn maxim about the story beginning when the conflict begins. "In other words," I explained, "until you have a conflict, you don't have a story."

I glanced past Eleanor and saw the other members of the group nodding in agreement or lost in meditations of their own. Brian and Kate sat together uncomfortably on the loveseat, keeping as far apart as they could. Sara and Josh occupied a pair of straight-backed chairs facing them, while I perched on a stool near the kitchen door. Eleanor herself sat huddled on a rickety armchair that creaked and swayed beside my halogen floor lamp. Everyone was there except Jackie, who was missing her first meeting since joining the group two months before. I admit I was a little relieved that Jackie had played hooky that night. She was bright and irreverent and when I invited her to join I expected her to add a little zest to the meetings. But as it turned out we got a little more zest and irreverence than I bargained for. In two months she had managed to antagonize everyone, even gentle Eleanor, whose main shortcoming as a writer was her inability to imagine conflict between her characters.

That night Eleanor's story began ploddingly as usual, describing her frustrations as the wife of a philandering husband and the mother of two selfish twenty-somethings. When I made my comment about the need for conflict, I had assumed that we were in for another self-pitying snooze fest. Nothing in the first few pages gave any hint of the chilling scenario that was about to fasten its grip on our lives.

Eleanor sat with her eyes cast down at the manuscript on her lap. "Bear with me," she murmured, flipping a few pages ahead. "Let me start a little further in."

And then, in tense, rising voice, she began to read: *"Margaret felt her anger taking control of her in a way she had never experienced before, jabbing in and out of her eyes, her mouth, her stomach, as if she were some poor soul snagged by demons in a Hieronymus Bosch painting…"*

It went on like that for twenty minutes, as Eleanor recounted Margaret's rage on finding an obscene photograph of her husband Robert with a blond younger woman who was undoubtedly his secretary at the bank. She raged against Robert, raged against her son and daughter—who showed insufficient concern when she was afraid she might have cancer—and raged against the other woman, whose shameless expression in the photograph triggered an emotion she had never felt before and couldn't name—"probably," Margaret thought, "because it came from God." It was much more than anger: it took her in its grip and shook her like a puppet and dragged her out the door of her apartment and into a cab headed downtown to the bank where Robert worked and when she found the blond woman she followed her home on the subway to a remote part of Queens, almost retching when she caught a whiff of the perfume Robert had given her for Christmas every year since they were married. On the elevated subway platform she reached in her purse and touched a letter opener she carried for protection when she went out by herself—it was about six inches long with a pearl handle and quite sharp at the tip—and it struck her that the woman probably knew her name. The idea that the woman knew her name filled Margaret with shame and indignant fury. That she might speak Margaret's name was an abomination. An abomination that would bring the wrath of God down on her head. They trudged several blocks down a crowded street that looked and smelled like a Middle Eastern bazaar and then turned into a side street lined with apartment buildings and shabby houses with children swarming in and out like flies. Margaret kept a tight grip on her purse but held it slightly open so she could touch the pearl handle of the letter opener. She was an instrument of divine retribution and she had to be ready when the call came. When the woman stepped up to a small house and put her key in the door, she turned to face Margaret and said Margaret's name, and Margaret followed her inside…

Eleanor's voice trailed off. "That's as far I've gotten."

The rest of us sat in stunned silence. Until that night we had scarcely heard Eleanor speak above a whisper, and suddenly here she was, shaking her fists and declaiming in Biblical tones about shame and retribution. It was as if she'd been taken over by some supernatural force. And although no one in the group would say so, we all knew where her outpouring of emotion was coming from. We had all been there the week before for Jackie's latest provocation, bleached-blond Jackie from Queens who came to our meetings directly from work every Tuesday night with the tale of her latest seduction of a married man. Jackie had read the latest installment of her quasi-pornographic memoirs, and even then it had seemed calculated to embarrass Eleanor, the only other married woman in the group. And where was Jackie now? Didn't she even have the decency to show up and face the consequences? No one would question her morals or sexual proclivities—we had an unwritten rule that no autobiographical inferences could be drawn from any member's work. Everything we wrote had to be taken as fiction, pure fiction, and all our labors were aimed at finding the truest expression for our falsehoods. Of course that rule was itself a fiction. We were about to find out whether it could survive in the brutal light of truth.

"Is that how the story ends?" Brian finally ventured to ask.

"I'm not sure," Eleanor muttered, keeping her eyes down. "It's a work in progress."

"It's incredibly powerful," said Kate, shoving Brian aside as she reached out to squeeze Eleanor's hand. "Incredibly powerful. You're tapping into the only genuine emotion that most women ever feel."

I knew the others were waiting to see how I would react. I didn't want to discourage Eleanor from getting more in touch with her emotions, but I had some reservations about what she had just read. "I'm still not hearing much conflict," I said tentatively. "Inner rage, yes, but that's not quite the same thing. We still don't know where the story is going, but so far Margaret has avoided any actual conflict."

Before Eleanor could respond, the buzzer rang from downstairs and gave us all a jolt. I hurried to the intercom and pushed the button. "Yes?"

"Police," came a man's voice. "Can I come up and speak with you, please?"

2

I'll admit I was not overjoyed at the prospect of welcoming New York's Finest into my living room. Though I support the police as firmly as the next man when they're arresting murderers, rapists or cigarette smokers, under ordinary conditions I prefer to keep them on the other side of the door. Now they were on their way upstairs and that old feeling of dread stirred inside me. Be polite, I told myself. Policemen are delicate creatures, as sensitive as your old Aunt Mary but armed to the teeth. You don't want to hurt their feelings.

By the way, my name is Will Schaefer and I'm 37 years old, single, white, heterosexual, kind to animals, with a keen enjoyment of literature, music and art (at least that's what it says in my listing on coolsingles.com). I donate generously to a number of worthy causes and strive to keep my carbon footprint well below actual shoe size. I started the writers' group with the best of intentions—contrary to my ex-girlfriend Zelda, who once accused me of starting it for the sole purpose of meeting women. There's some truth in that, though most of the women in the group have been more like Eleanor than anyone I'd ever go out with. Sara was the big exception, but that night when the police knocked on my door I had only the faintest glimmering of what she would mean to my life.

It was the second week of June in what would prove to be the hottest summer on record. New York, America, the whole world seemed to be tottering on the brink of catastrophe, as if suddenly in our progress from the Big Bang to extinction we had reached the tipping point. The economy—what was left of it—was crashing, the glaciers melting, the politicians running for cover. My job at Zunax Corporation had taken on a surrealistic quality as the first whiffs of suspicion about the company's finances began to swirl through the internet, and on Wall Street the indictment of Paul Gratzky had called into question the basic economic assumptions of the age. Gratzky was the Einstein of modern finance and his Hermetica Fund was regarded as proof that he had found the Holy Grail. No one knew how he did it except his "quants"—the mathematical geniuses he recruited from Princeton and MIT—but his hedge fund had prospered with returns in the high double digits under all kinds of conditions, surviving even the disastrous meltdowns and bailouts of the past few years. Now the government claimed it was all a giant Ponzi scheme. The enormity of the charges and their potential consequences had thrown the financial markets into a state of suspended shock. Ordinary New Yorkers went through their usual motions like sleepwalkers as they waited for the latest catastrophe to unfold. Even the weather stopped its restless gyrations and clamped the entire continent into a torturous stranglehold, with temperatures from Seattle to Key West simmering in the mid-90s for weeks. The unexpected, the outrageous, the unthinkable—all the improbabilities Gratzky had been able to arbitrage against each other for decades—suddenly seemed capable of happening at once. Our perfect world, it turned out, was a mosaic of imperfections, pregnant with conflict and change. And rough beasts by the thousands slouched in the streets of New York, waiting for their hour to come round at last.

I stood waiting at the door until a stocky, dark-haired man in a brown suit glided off the elevator and headed toward my apartment. His tie hung loose around his neck, dangling over a sweat-soaked shirt. He had a pock-marked face and a pair of unforgiving eyes that made me glad I stayed on the right side of the law.

"Mr. Schaefer?" he queried as he stepped toward me.

"That's me. How can I help you?"

He held up a badge in a folding leather case. "Detective Albert Falcone, NYPD. May I come in?"

"Is something the matter?"

"It's brutal out here," he replied, as if in answer to my question. "May I come in?"

"Sure."

I didn't like the way he was looking at me but I had no choice but to invite him inside. The group sat in dead silence but when he saw them staring back at him he registered no surprise. "It's about Jacqueline Barkocy," he said in a low voice.

"She didn't come tonight. Is something the matter?"

"Were you expecting her?"

"Of course. Is something the matter?"

He hesitated, sizing me up with his cold eyes. "Yes, I'm afraid so." One of the women in the group gasped and started to sob. "Then you haven't heard?"

"Heard what?"

"Ms. Barkocy was stabbed to death in her home last Thursday. June the ninth."

"Jackie Barkocy?"

"It was an apparent robbery attempt," he said evenly. "No arrest has been made."

"I can't believe this."

"I thought you would have heard by now. Wasn't she a friend of yours?"

"Yes, though I haven't known her very long. I don't think any of us have. She was our newest member." I glanced around at the others, but no one spoke, so preoccupied were they with their own emotions. Eleanor sobbed and gasped for breath while Brian mopped his brow with a handkerchief, his eyes rolling desperately behind his black-rimmed glasses. Sara frowned with an air of disbelief. Kate glared back fiercely at the policeman, as if his bringing us this news was a act of predictable brutality. Only Josh seemed to be measuring the situation objectively, calculating, behind his dark eyes, a swift and stern retribution. "She came to the meetings religiously," I added. "I don't think she ever missed one."

"What is this? Are you some kind of a therapist?"

"No. It's a writers' group. Jackie's been a member for the past two or three months." Then all at once I wondered why I was submitting to this interrogation. "How did you know to come here?" I asked.

"You were on her calendar for every Tuesday night," he said, softening his tone. "Including tonight."

Detective Falcone stayed for almost an hour, interviewing each of us separately as he stood in the kitchen taking notes on a clipboard without sitting down. He was a serious man who never smiled or raised his voice above a bureaucratic monotone. He did not shed his suit jacket or loosen his tie even though it was 96 degrees outside and the air conditioner was struggling mightily with a roomful of overwrought people. In the course of these interviews he answered most of our questions about Jackie's death. On that Thursday afternoon—two days after she'd read her story to the group—she left her office at five o'clock and walked the few blocks to her usual subway stop, where she was observed by a co-worker boarding the train to Queens. Apparently she took the train to her usual stop because she was again observed in Queens, this time by a neighbor, walking in the direction of her home. The killer must have waited inside the house or followed her immediately through the door, because when her body was found she was wearing her work clothes, which she always changed as soon as she came home from the office. She was stabbed multiple times around the neck and throat with a sharp instrument that was not found. Her empty purse lay on the floor, as did the keys she had just used to open the door. A small private funeral had taken place on the weekend.

I threw together some cold drinks while Detective Falcone questioned each member of the group. Sara, lithe and beautiful, was of course the first to catch his eye. She gave him as little information as possible, answering even the most perfunctory questions with an elusive shrug. I watched them out of the corner of my eye with just a twinge of jealousy as I served the drinks to the others. In spite of Sara's minimalist approach, Detective Falcone seemed grateful for her attention, and after a few minutes he moved on to Josh. Josh always came to meetings in a black suit, as if he were returning from a funeral (though of course it was only his job at the insurance company). His raven hair and fathomless eyes projected an air of tragic inevitability that must have seemed promising to the detective. The two of them conferred at close range in a somber undertone for several minutes, the detective taking copious notes. Meanwhile Brian, also in the suit he'd worn to work, stood a few steps to one side, wiping the sweat from his forehead as he tried to keep his heavy glasses from sliding down his nose. He was the only African-American in the group and the presence of the policeman seemed to make him uncomfortable, possibly because he felt vibrations of hostility or suspicion that were not aimed at the rest of us. Eleanor remained seated in the living room, still wheezing and sobbing; ironically, the detective spent the least amount of time questioning her.

Kate, who was a social worker and a militant feminist, had come to the meeting in her usual jeans and sandals, braless in a T-shirt commemorating some march in Central Park. She listened to Detective Falcone with an expression of skepticism that reflected her attitude toward the police. "What about Larry?" I heard her ask.

"Larry?"

"Jackie's husband. Did he find the body?"

"No. The husband was out of town. The door was left standing open and one of the kids from the neighborhood went in and found the body."

"Then Larry isn't a suspect?"

Detective Falcone hesitated. "I shouldn't answer that since there's been no official statement. But I'll tell you this: the husband was at a meeting in Chicago with about a hundred people at the time the stabbing occurred."

Finally it was my turn to be questioned, and by this time I had to force myself to be cooperative. Detective Falcone looked like the kind of cop who'd do anything to put another notch on his belt. There was something insinuating about the way he stared at me, rolling his words slowly around on his lips as if he had evidence he was deliberately holding back, evidence I was well aware of and undoubtedly trying to conceal. The tone of his questioning was unmistakable: we were all considered potential suspects, and if there was a way we could all be guilty he was determined to find it. Listening to him brought out a protective streak I'd discovered in myself as a child when I defended my younger siblings from a drunken, abusive father. Now the writers' group was my family and I had to do everything in my power to protect it— whether from the sharp instruments of a killer or the blunt machinery of the law. I knew I had the strength inside me to do the right thing. But I felt almost queasy with the conflicting loyalties and fears that would haunt me for weeks to come: Was the enemy out there—or was it right here in my apartment?

When he had finished questioning me, Detective Falcone raised his voice so that everyone could hear him. "I want to thank you all for your cooperation." It was the beginning of a speech he had given many times before, but before continuing he asked me in an aside, "Is everyone here tonight? Is this the whole group?"

"All except Jackie," I said.

He nodded grimly and went back to his speech. "Again, thanks for your cooperation. I have your names and contact information and may be reaching out to you again if necessary. In the meantime, I gave each of you a card with my name and contact information. If you think of anything you think might be helpful, please leave a message on my cell phone and I'll get right back to you."

3

After my first year in New York, I still felt like a fish out of water. The mile-a-minute pace, the obsession with money, the deafening roar of eight million egos swarming in such a small space, were pushing me farther and farther into myself. Sure, I had friends, but most of them were a little too rich and full of themselves, or a little too envious and cynical, to be counted on when I needed them. I'd quit my job as an English teacher in Houston to start the life I'd dreamed about since I was a boy, yet here I was a year later, lonely, bored out of my skull writing corporate press releases and coming to the realization that unless I won the lottery I'd never be able to do anything else. I was drinking too much, paralyzed by writer's block, slipping away from the humanism that had drawn me to literature in the first place. So I volunteered to teach an adult education course in fiction writing at the Y. When the semester ended, I suggested that the class continue as an informal writers' group, meeting every Tuesday night at my apartment in Chelsea. Not that I had any particular qualifications to be the leader, other than a desire to help people follow their dreams. But wasn't that enough? To help others discover new worlds in their own distinctive voices— could there be a more affirmative way to survive in the Babel of modern life? What harm could come of the attempt?

I should have known better. As long as I could remember I'd been a hostage to the botched lives of my alcoholic parents. They taught, by their example, the arts of evasion and deception, instilling a lifelong dread of exposure—the gnawing fear that sooner or later the truth would come out. I tried to escape by finding a new family that had nothing to hide, and that's what the writers' group became: a family. Not necessarily a happy one—those are all alike, aren't they?—but a family nevertheless. And until this year the group was everything I hoped it would be: an island of order and humanity in a world of intensifying chaos and dehumanization. It was the only part of my life I really cared about.

Then Jackie joined the group, and after a harsh winter and a difficult spring things started to go terribly wrong. And I began to feel again that gnawing sense of dread I grew up with. It was as if an old enemy had tracked me down.

After Detective Falcone left we all sat silently in a state of shock. Sara buried her face in her hands, Brian stared down at his laptop, Josh pawed nervously through the books on the shelf beside the couch. Kate frowned at me as if she expected me to say it was all a mistake. No one said what we were all thinking: that Eleanor, in the story she had just read, had practically confessed to following Jackie home on the train with the murder weapon in her purse. But the idea that Eleanor might have killed Jackie was so unthinkable that no one could even mumble the stock phrases that usually spring to mind on such occasions.

Eleanor herself looked pale and sick, as if she was ready to faint. She fumbled for her cell phone and called her husband, who always came to pick her up after our meetings. I couldn't hear exactly what she murmured into the phone, but I assumed she was asking him to come earlier than usual.

"Well," I finally said, "let's call it a night. There's no point in trying to talk about this or anything else tonight. We'll try again next week."

They all nodded and stood up to gather their things, limiting their good-byes to a muted sob or a quick hug as they stumbled out the door. Eleanor lingered behind, waiting for her husband, and we shared a few awkward moments as each of us reiterated our prior expressions of shock and disbelief without venturing beyond them.

"Will you carry on with the writers' group?" she asked, daubing her tears with a handkerchief.

"Absolutely. We have to stick together at a time like this."

"That's right. We have to stick together." She made a brave smile and reached out to squeeze my hand. Her grip felt so thin, so innocent, that I wanted to cradle her in my arms. That was not a murderer's hand, I told myself. There had to be another ending to the story.

Finally the downstairs buzzer rang and I escorted Eleanor down the elevator to the entrance foyer, where her husband Howard stood waiting at the door. I knew Howard from my day job at Zunax. He was an old college friend of our CEO, Milton Babst, and did some kind of consulting work for the company—in fact that was how Eleanor had been introduced to the group—but I can't say I was ever glad to see him. Pudgy and red-cheeked beneath his sparsely etched hairline, he was the sort of sixty-year-old man you might describe as "portly" if you were selling him a suit or "heavy-set" if he was marrying your sister, but for everyday purposes I'd have to say he was just plain fat, with a little moustache and an air of misplaced vanity that made him look like Oliver Hardy. It was hard to believe that Eleanor was worried about losing him to another woman.

"I hope you haven't been telling tales out of school," he chuckled, as he always did when he came to pick her up. Evidently his biggest fear was that his wife might tell the truth about him.

"Not tonight, Howard," Eleanor moaned. "Jackie's been murdered."

The color faded from Howard's cheeks faster than a politician's smile. After questioning me for the details, he put his arm around Eleanor and helped her out to the cab he'd left waiting at the curb. I gave her hand a squeeze as she silently turned to face me before stumbling away.

"Good night, Will," Howard murmured, with a glance over his shoulder. "Thanks for bringing her downstairs."

On my way back upstairs I passed my ex-girlfriend Zelda's apartment and heard a distinct growling sound coming through the door. It might have been Zelda's gray weimaraner Wolfgang—a high-strung refugee from the Humane Society whose body was covered with hideous, supposedly benign growths—or it might have been Zelda herself, who'd never quite got over our relationship and its unhappy ending. Six months earlier she'd stormed out of my life and barricaded herself in her apartment with Wolfgang, peppering me with nasty emails, anonymous phone calls and notes tacked to my door that demanded the return of toiletries, transit passes and all the Christmas and birthday presents she'd ever given me. I tried to maintain an amicable relationship but she seemed determined to hate me. Significantly it was the writers' group—or rather her jealousy aroused by the time and attention I devoted to it—that triggered our final breakup. Zelda was a physics major turned Wall Street quant with no interest in literature or the arts other than death metal music inflicted by garage bands in Brooklyn and Jersey City. The longer we knew each other the more I realized we had absolutely nothing in common—a flaw in our relationship which, in spite of her braininess, Zelda never noticed for herself, and to which, when I pointed it out, she reacted in an explosively unforgiving fashion. With her bad temper and her spiky orange hair it was a wonder she could hold a job on Wall Street, other than the fact that she was a mathematical genius. Before I met her she'd worked for Paul Gratzky as one of the gnomes pulling levers at the Hermetica Fund, and evidently there was more to their relationship than crunching numbers. That relationship too had ended badly: not only had Gratzky fired her, he'd broken her heart, and she enjoyed predicting his imminent collapse. And although I had no reason to suspect any connection, in the past week the anonymous phone calls had started again. My house phone would ring in the middle of the night—just once, but enough to wake me up—and when I answered all I heard was a dial tone. No heavy breathing, no threats, just silence: that was Zelda's way of letting me know she was still there. And now as I walked past her door I heard the growling, and I hoped with all my heart that it was Wolfgang.

Back in my apartment, I sat for a while listening to the struggling air conditioner and then poured myself a Jack Daniel's, hoping it would settle my nerves so I could go to sleep. In the privacy of my own thoughts I was able to think less guardedly about what had happened to Jackie, and Eleanor's possible role in it. It was a hard conversation to have, even with myself, about people I thought of as family.

What did I really know about Eleanor? I asked myself. What did any of us in the group really know about each other? Of course I knew a little more than the others, since part of my responsibility was to select the members, but even the information I had about them was only what they told me. Eleanor, like Margaret in her story, lived on the East Side and devoted most of her time to charity work. I was acquainted with her husband Howard, but only in the context of Zunax, where I knew that most of what I thought I knew was false. Howard had learned about the group from my boss, Bob Tedder; he asked me, dropping Bob's name, if his wife could become a member. She was a serious writer, he said, trying to get her stories into print. I was annoyed with Bob for putting me in this position, but my misgivings vanished when I met Eleanor and read some of her work. She painted an appealing picture of herself in her stories, as she did in real life. She seemed gentle, humane, quaintly troubled by the brutality of the modern world—until now, when she'd shown us an alternative possibility in her furious fantasy about the betrayed wife she called Margaret. How much of that story was Eleanor and how much was Margaret? I had no way of knowing.

That was true as well for the other members of the group. Brian was a mild-mannered engineer specializing in office-building security systems and emergency logistics. I met him when his company was installing an alarm system in the Zunax building. He noticed *War and Peace* on my desk and we chatted amiably about literature and writing, which described as his passions in life. He was an African-American whose two young children lived with his ex-wife, and in his empty evenings and weekends he wrote stories of sex and violence that he probably would not have wanted his children to read. His writing, as he described it, was his road not taken, a visit to a planet he might still inhabit if his mother had not mustered enough determination to push him through Bronx Science and on to Hunter College. He wrote about pimps and whores and corrupt cops in the blasted crackscape of the South Bronx, as seen through the eyes of Lieutenant Val Osbourne, a man much like himself, brave but intellectual and ambivalent about his place in the world. At least that's what I thought I knew about Brian. But how much did I really know?

Kate was a feminist, unmarried at 35, who worked at a shelter for battered immigrant women. Her job provided a wealth of material—abduction, slavery, prostitution, violence—and in her writing she professed unflinching realism. But ironically her stories, though grounded in the most painful experiences, had an air of unreality, possibly because in her severity she left no room for that most human of failings, the ability to adapt to suffering and even to laugh at it. Her own life, as far as anyone could tell, had been totally benign, unless you consider an Irish Catholic upbringing on Staten Island to be a form of abuse. She was tall, red-haired and haughty, with more than a speck of flint in her eyes. I thought I knew her—I even took her out to dinner once—but that was only because I'd known plenty of other women like her. As I thought about it, I realized that my image of Kate was based more on what I knew about those other women than on what I knew about her. One thing I was sure of: she'd been introduced to me by Zelda. I wished I could remember how Zelda knew her.

Josh was the only member of the group whose writing made no attempt at realism. His stories were the Kafkaesque fantasies of a 30-year-old man who still lived at home, unable to escape the stifling blandishments of his mother or the demeaning machinations of his father. The stories were bizarre and often quite funny but there was nothing in them that revealed anything about Josh's life. All I really knew about him was his address in Brooklyn and the fact that he worked as an actuary for an insurance company.

That leaves Sara. Sara was elegant and beautiful, with short black hair and luminous skin and a lithe, effortless way of standing still, like a ballet dancer. The first time I saw her I had a presentiment of the fascination she would come to exert over me. She had come to my apartment with a typewritten manuscript as a sample of her work. The style was spare, minimalist almost to the point of negation, and I had a difficult time grasping what was happening in the story. But beneath its hard surface the story had a beating heart, a humanity that spoke volumes about the person who had written it. I glanced up from my reading and for a brief moment glimpsed the wry smile that had formed on her lips as she watched my struggle to understand her story. The smile quickly vanished, but that moment has epitomized our relationship ever since. I sensed that the minimalism of her writing was the reflection of an elusive persona, a riddle she would ask in a thousand ways but never answer. I questioned her for over an hour and read more of her stories and I did learn a few things about her. She was the youngest daughter of a heart surgeon who had emigrated from Chile when she was a small child, along with her mother and three older siblings. She grew up in New Jersey and attended Yale, taking her degree in art history, and now she worked for a large publishing conglomerate publicizing art books. But none of this mattered, I realized. All that mattered were the things she didn't tell me, the secrets beneath the mirror-like surface that she knew I could never grasp.

Sara's Journal
June 14

Jackie is dead and I feel sick inside. Everyone's in a state of shock. You don't know how to feel, how to act. It's like you're watching yourself in a movie as you go through the motions. Why did that cop show up during the group meeting? He must think one of us killed her.

I promised myself I'd get this journal going again. Will says write about your life, write about what you see and do every day. What I see every day is Mom dying of cancer. What I do is go to the nursing home to watch her and try not to spend too much time crying. Not much to write about or even to call a life. I feel like an empty shell, smooth on the outside and dark in the middle.

This is going to take—I hate to say it—courage. Something I don't usually expect of myself. Mom asked me to pray for her, which I will do if it makes her feel better. I hope somebody's praying for me.

4

Continuation by Will Schaefer

It was characteristic of Jackie to bare her innermost secrets like bullets in a Power Point presentation. Yet she too was an enigma in her own way. At our last meeting it had been her turn to read. Everyone seemed a little on edge because her stories always mocked or attacked at least one member of the group, usually whoever had criticized her the last time. But what seemed to bother people most was her subject matter. She was a serial adulteress, a stalker of married men. At least that's how she portrayed herself in her stories, which no one in the group doubted were fragments of a vast pornographic autobiography. The heroine—though she might be called Leslie or Lisa or Jessica—always looked and sounded like a younger, hipper version of Jackie. Her lover was invariably a married man, usually rich, often unfaithful, but never cruel or dishonorable. Marriage for Jackie had lost none of its ancient mystique. A married man, a man who had committed himself to a woman—especially a different woman—stood out as a mythic figure in her eyes, a knight on a quest for some unattainable goal. Only a married man could be what she needed in a hero: a complete man who could guide her down the mean streets of love without himself being mean, a man brave and cheerful yet saddened by his knowledge of the inevitable unhappy ending. Not that there was anything uplifting or noble about it. In her last story she had portrayed

herself as a young widow who once a week would leave her
two small children with a babysitter and take the train to JFK
Airport, where she would pick up a married man almost at
random and spend the night with him in his hotel room.

The only married man Jackie wasn't interested in was her
husband, a spineless, clueless eunuch who was usually named
Larry. We all knew Larry as well as if he'd been a member of
the group. He was skinny and bespectacled and self-effacing
to the point of invisibility, with enough nervous tics to wear
out a small mime troop. He taught algebra and business
math at a high school in Queens, where he also coached the
chess club. At home he wore cardigan sweaters and corduroy
slippers and spent his spare time solving chess problems and
watching the Mets and the Rangers on TV, never wondering
why his wife had to work so much overtime and sleep over at
her mother's so often. The couple had no children and
perhaps that was the source of Jackie's obsessive search for
another kind of happiness.

I thought back to that last meeting, just a week before.
Jackie had seemed more aggressive than usual, more sarcastic,
more determined to antagonize the group. She pulled out her
manuscript and waited for everyone to be settled in their
seats before she began to read, clearing her throat impatiently,
sweeping her imperious gaze across the group to command
our undivided attention. But when she read it was in a voice,
unlike her usual voice, that sounded feminine and vulnerable
and permanently out of breath.

"*I felt like the heroine of some third-rate romance,*" she began,
and she recounted the travails of a legal secretary named
Leslie, enmeshed in an unsatisfactory affair with her boss
Jeffrey, a married attorney. Longing to escape from Jeffrey,
Leslie finds her opportunity with a wealthy Argentine banker,

deceiving not only Jeffrey but her husband, the feckless Larry, whom she describes as the World's Most Clueless Man. The Argentine—named Claudio—entertains her in a sumptuous love nest on Gramercy Park under the watchful eye of his bodyguard, a young black man named Dale who is described as a "security expert." To Leslie the luxury and intrigue are exciting, almost intoxicating. She feels like a queen bee, freed from captivity, basking in the attention of compliant men and only vaguely aware of the honeycomb of secrets being constructed around her.

One morning she and Claudio meet for sex on the pretense of preparing documents for a real-estate closing. Later, when they arrive at Claudio's favorite restaurant for lunch, they find his usual table occupied by his icy, unattractive wife and their three college-age children: Alexandra, the "evil" daughter, who attends Princeton and is "dressed like a French whore"; Francesca, described as "retarded," who works in a soup kitchen for disabled African AIDS widows and frets over the suffering women of the world; and Michael, who searches for the meaning of life playing video games and surfing the internet. Claudio introduces Leslie as Jeffrey's secretary but the wife and the daughters are not deceived. They taunt her condescendingly, and when lunch is over they clamber into the limousine driven by the bodyguard Dale and accompany Claudio and Leslie back to Jeffrey's law firm, where the wife precipitates a bitter confrontation. She exposes both of Leslie's affairs— the affair with Claudio and the one with Jeffrey—and when Jeffrey tries to deny her, Leslie is infuriated. Jeffrey fires her on the spot and asks Dale to escort her out of the building. On the way outside, Dale makes a play for her and she notices, for the first time, what a beautiful specimen of manhood he is. Why had she been wasting the best years of her life on a nerdball like Jeffrey and a charlatan like Claudio?

And so they slip back into the limousine and drive to a hotel, stopping on the way to buy a bottle of vodka. They start drinking as soon as they step into their room, laughing at Jeff and Claudio and Larry as they undress. Leslie looks forward excitedly to an altogether new experience—her first time with a black man—but unfortunately the vodka has the opposite effect on Dale. By the time they are ready to join forces he is *hors de combat* and soon falls sound asleep. She shoves her clothes back on and slips outside, knowing that the only thing more humiliating than what has already happened that day was what was likely to happen next. After wandering the streets for a couple of hours she finds her way to Grand Central Station, where she catches a train home to Queens.

Larry doesn't seem to notice her dishabille or the vodka on her breath or her general state of existential despair. "Will you look at this?" he shouts when she plods through the door. "The Mets are blowing another one!"

I expected that Jackie's story would trigger a spirited discussion. It's customary to start with a compliment, something you liked about the story as a springboard for suggestions about how it could be improved, but on this occasion no one seemed willing to offer anything but a blank stare. Looking back now, I wish we'd left it at that. But in fact the story had stirred up latent hostilities and left some members of the group spoiling for a fight. After all it wasn't exactly a bedtime story.

"I liked the way you conveyed an almost medieval atmosphere at the beginning with the dungeon metaphor," I began, sounding a positive note. "It sets up the story as a kind of romance."

Jackie nodded and smiled.

"If you think holding women in captivity is romantic," said Kate.

"And after a couple of paragraphs," Sara added before Jackie could respond, "the metaphor just sort of melts away. The story seems to morph into something different."

"That's the whole point," Jackie said, puckering her face in Sara's direction.

"Oh," said Kate. "Is *that* the point?"

When it became clear that this debate had run its course—with Sara, Kate and Jackie all staring at me to avoid looking at each other—I waded in with a criticism of my own. "I'm troubled by your relationship to your characters," I told Jackie. "Other than the narrator, of course. It's something about your writing you should work on."

"You think I have to *like* my characters?"

"No, but you do have to love them."

I knew that would get the group's attention, and what I said next was even more provocative. "You can be a mediocre writer," I said, addressing the group as a whole, "even a successful one, by creating a varied set of characters and then holding them up to ridicule or disdain. Tom Wolfe comes to mind. But if you want to be a good writer or a great writer you have to love your characters the way God loves his creatures."

"God?" Jackie was sputtering with incredulity. "Are you saying I have to believe in God to be a writer?"

"Not at all," I smiled. "You can believe or not believe in God, as you choose. But you have to be able to see your characters through the eyes of whatever God you believe or don't believe in. And you have to care about them the same way that he or she would."

A long silence ensued, during which I tried to make up for my excursion into theology by passing a plate of cookies around the room.

"I agree," Brian finally said. "That's what makes Tolstoy the greatest of all novelists. He loves his characters, even the bad ones."

"Especially the bad ones," Kate nodded. "They say God loves a sinner more than any saint."

"Christ! What a load of crap!" Jackie snorted, perching forward in her chair as if preparing to launch out of it. "Doesn't anybody have anything worthwhile to say about this story?"

She cast her eyes around the room defiantly.

"Yes, I do," Brian finally said. "At least I hope you'll think it's worthwhile. To be quite honest, I was offended by the stereotype of the African-American security guard."

"Oh, come on!"

"He's a shiftless servant, a street criminal and an alcoholic, and he lusts after a white woman who fantasizes about his body as if he belonged to some other species. Forgive me if I missed any other racist stereotypes you might have sneaked into the story."

Jackie shook her head in a pantomime of disbelief. "How about being impotent? Is that a racist stereotype?"

"No, it's a counter-stereotype, which is almost as bad."

Brian had made some good points, and I was glad he felt comfortable raising them in the group. But I think there was another, unmentioned reason why he felt the need to speak up. Jackie had identified Dale, the black man in the story, as a "security expert," which was how Brian described himself when asked about his own occupation. In fact Brian was a security expert of a much higher order: he supervised the design and installation of security systems in office buildings. But by giving Dale the same job title, Jackie had equated Brian with an untrustworthy, alcoholic—and impotent—chauffeur. It was inflammatory, to say the least, and I decided it was time to move the discussion in a different direction.

"In general it's a good idea to avoid attributing the characters' prejudices and opinions to the author," I said. "Unless of course"—I raised my eyebrows at Jackie—"they represent the views of the author."

"Absolutely not," she sniffed. "I don't have a racist bone in my body."

"There are other offensive stereotypes in the story," Sara said crisply. "The idea that the daughter was evil just because she went to Princeton, or that she was evil at all, when all she was trying to do was defend her family from a woman who was obviously trying to destroy them."

We all knew where this was coming from: Sara herself had graduated from Yale and she enjoyed a close relationship with her own mother, who had recently been in chemotherapy. But I think it was the description of Alexandra as being dressed like a French whore that triggered her reaction. Sara's clothes were always tasteful and understated.

"Or that the other daughter was *retarded*," growled Kate. "I can't believe you would use that expression the way you did. And what makes her so retarded? Because she was trying to get the other characters to acknowledge the abuse women face in this world every day of their lives?"

For some reason Kate looked at Josh, as if for support, even though she usually seemed to despise him. It must have been because in the story he'd played the role of Michael, her good-for-nothing brother. "Ahhh," Josh hesitated, dipping his dark brow toward Kate. "I don't know."

"I know," said Eleanor, in a voice so soft we all had to stop rustling our papers to hear her. "I know why you wrote that story." There was something eerie about her whistling voice and the gleam her eyes caught from my halogen lamp. "You wrote that story to tell me what you would like to do with my husband."

5

The night Detective Falcone came to my apartment with the news of Jackie's death was one of the longest nights of my life. Our meeting broke up at 9:30, with Kate and Sara still sobbing as they stumbled out to the street. Even at that hour the temperature was still about ninety, with enough humidity in the air to float a battleship. My air conditioner put up a valiant struggle, but in the end I had no choice but to open the windows and pray for a breeze that never came. Seven floors above street level my bedroom window opened on an air shaft, but what came in was more noise than air, and the sickening smell of a summer gone bad. Across the roofscape marched a sinister army of elevated water tanks that looked like aliens from an old science fiction movie.

For a couple of hours I drank Jack Daniel's and brooded about Jackie and Eleanor and the others, asking myself what was going to happen to the writers' group. One of us was dead, another might have killed her. How could the group survive? And what should I do to protect it? No matter what I did I would be betraying someone. The old enemy was back: that sense of dread I had grown up with—the fear not of evil itself but of its exposure to the light. Finally about midnight I went out and walked up and down 23rd Street where the bars were trying to come to life. I thought about stepping into Rumpelstiltskin for an Irish coffee but ended up floating in the fog down to the Village and then back on Broadway to my apartment, which was still as stuffy as when

I left it. A couple more shots of Jack Daniel's and a cold shower and I'd be ready to sweat myself to sleep. It was 4:00 a.m. and I had to be at work in five hours.

As I was pouring my nightcap I made what I thought was an inconsequential discovery. Someone in the group had left a paperback book on the end table near the door. I recognized the book—it was *And Then There Were None*, by Agatha Christie—and a quick glance confirmed that it was my own copy, which I must have loaned to one of the members. I couldn't recall who had borrowed it. It's the classic tale about a group of strangers who come to an island off the coast of England for a brief vacation and are murdered, one after the other, by a psychopath—a member of the group, as I recalled—who has gathered them there for that purpose. Not the best topic of discussion on that particular night, which probably explained why the borrower had simply left it on the table. I thought nothing of it at the time, merely making a mental note, as I jammed the book into place on my shelf of paperback mysteries, to bring it up at a later meeting.

Then, as I was undressing, something happened that sent a little jolt through my tired brain. The telephone rang, stopping before I could pick it up. It was my land line, the number I kept solely for calls I didn't want. Caller ID identified my torturer simply as Private Caller, as it had always done, but I knew it could only be Zelda. As if growling through the door wasn't enough on a night like this. The only thing different about the call, which I scarcely noticed, was that now there were two rings instead of one.

I was awoken at eight o'clock by an urgent broadcast advising the young, the aged, the pregnant, and those who suffered from allergies, asthma and other respiratory disorders to stay inside and avoid breathing if at all possible. A cloud of yellow aspic had gelled over the city during the night, turning it into a monstrous petri dish of disease and suffocation. Those few citizens who didn't fit into one of the protected categories were expected to take a deep breath and go to work. I showered and dressed, bolting down a cinnamon bun and a glass of orange juice before rushing out of my apartment. Halfway down the hall I passed Zelda's door, alert to signs of hostility, but I heard no growling, no TV, no running water, not the faintest echo of Zelda or Wolfgang. The two of them were probably out decorating the neighborhood with dog turds, for which neither acknowledged any responsibility. I ran back to my apartment and jotted down a curt note which I taped to the door as I passed the second time: "Your phone calls are getting annoying. If you have something to say please say it."

I confess I indulged in some evil thoughts about Zelda as I rode down on the elevator. Her former boss, Paul Gratzky, had made billions but he'd paid a steep price for his success. He and his family were plagued with disasters—freak accidents, rare diseases, bizarre crimes—and now, according to the *Daily News*, a similar curse was beginning to afflict his employees and business associates. One of the computer programmers at Hermetica had fallen from a tenth story window while acting out a fantasy from Second Life, and another colleague had succumbed to mad cow disease. Why couldn't something like that happen to Zelda? I asked myself, wondering if the curse had spread to Gratzky's ex-employees. Why couldn't she be attacked by wolves or come down with the bubonic plague? Naturally I felt guilty just thinking such thoughts, but I was fed up with her harassment and I assured myself that mere thought is never a crime. Still, nothing could be more unlucky than to wish for someone's death, especially a former girlfriend. It's a good thing, I told myself as I stepped outside—it's a good thing I'm not superstitious.

It was only a matter of time before I would be drawn into the widening orbit of the Gratzky curse. My employer, Zunax Corporation ("a Fortune 500 company offering breakthrough solutions in a web-based universe"), was connected to Gratzky through his lifelong friendship with our CEO, Milton Babst. Zunax has since achieved a notoriety surpassed only by Congress, but at that time it stood at the peak of its success. I worked as a senior director in the Public Affairs department and I'm ashamed to admit that I wrote many of the press releases that molded the company's public image. The inspiration for those essays I owe to my boss, Bob Tedder, Vice President of Public Affairs, a man whose genius for deception would have shocked Machiavelli. Outwardly a bland corporate sycophant, he was a master of self-promotion who had advanced to the highest level without taking any responsibility or doing any work, a virtuoso of unaccountability who never left his fingerprints on a document that wasn't headed for the shredder or made a decision that couldn't be attributed to someone else. He infuriated me but I had to admire the man. Not only was he phenomenally successful, but he had found a way—in violation of one of the company's most sacrosanct policies— to enjoy the favors of countless female employees of all races, colors and creeds, some of them higher than himself on the corporate ladder and some wriggling upwards through their association with him. How did he get away with it? People asked that question all the time, tirelessly debating the fine

points of every conceivable answer, but no one ever came
close to suspecting the truth. The connection between Bob
Tedder and Paul Gratzky—and thus the connection between
Gratzky and myself—would be revealed only in the fullness
of time.

Zunax's global headquarters stood at the corner of 39th
and Lexington, a brisk thirty-minute walk from my
apartment. On the morning after Detective Falcone
informed us of Jackie's death, the city was steaming like a rain
forest and the air tasted like cotton candy. I was a sweaty
mess by the time I reached the office. The first person I
encountered was Martin, my assistant, who stood huddled
over the photocopier with a sheaf of papers in one hand and
a *molto grande* cup of coffee in the other. Martin's job was to
assist me in correcting his typing errors, scheduling his
vacations, and resolving his elaborate disputes with the other
employees. Other than that—and a pervasive atmosphere of
paranoia and impending doom—I was never quite sure what
he added to my life. I had no idea why he'd be photocopying
files at that hour of the morning.

"You're not going to believe what she did this time," he
said as he followed me into my office.

"Who?"

"Helen. Who else?" Helen was one of the other
assistants, a tall black woman with a lopsided smile and an
interest in herbal remedies. I found her very pleasant but for
some reason she was Martin's nemesis. "She used up all the
toner for the color printer and didn't order any more. Now I
have to run down to Staples and buy some."

"Okay," I said, grateful for the chance to get some work
done. "Why don't you go to the downtown store?
Everything's a lot cheaper there."

"Sure, whatever you say." He stood in the doorway, examining me critically. I realized I'd forgotten to shave. "Bad night with the writers' group?"

"No," I lied, regretting it immediately. "Well, actually, yes. One of the members was murdered."

"Murdered? You're kidding!"

"Is that something I'd be kidding about?"

"No, sorry." He raised his arms in a pantomime of self-defense. "Just be sure to let me know who it was so I can take them off the contacts list."

The writers' group was a sore point with Martin. He had asked me if he could join and after some hesitation I agreed to read one of his stories, which only confirmed what I already knew: he was lazy, incompetent and about as creative as the average cedar post. When I cautiously suggested that he should take an introductory writing course, he stalked out of my office and spent the rest of the week deleting my incoming emails before I could read them. That was six months ago and he had long since moved on to other resentments, usually involving Helen or the company's sick-leave policy, which unaccountably required employees to be sick in order to qualify for its benefits.

Before he left for Staples, Martin passed on an interesting tidbit he'd gleaned from his perusal of the *Times*, which typically occupied the first hour or two of his work day. He was obsessed with the Gratzky case and made it a point to give me daily briefings on its progress. That morning's paper carried a story describing the prosecution's theory of the case for the first time. According to the U.S. Attorney, the Hermetica Fund traded simultaneously through supercomputers in markets all over the world, making as many as nine billion trades a day. The speed of the trades was such that they were virtually simultaneous, effectively allowing assets to be sold before they'd been bought, or at least before anyone knew they were missing, and then sold and bought again, with the process being repeated thousands of times within the space of a minute or less. Somehow this allowed the fund to make an enormous amount of money.

"Then what makes it a Ponzi scheme?" I wondered aloud. "Isn't that what they called it when Gratzky was indicted?"

"Yes," Martin agreed, "that's what they called it."

"But what you just described isn't a Ponzi scheme. In a Ponzi scheme you keep the investors happy by paying out fake earnings which is really the money coming in from new investors."

"Is that how it works?"

"The Hermetica Fund has been closed to new investors for years. So how could it be a Ponzi scheme?"

"Oh, I wouldn't know," Martin said with a peculiar smile. "I really wouldn't know about that. But I will say this." He lowered his voice and glanced over his shoulder to make sure no one was listening. "Now that Gratzky's been indicted, all these unexplained drownings and overdoses and fatal one-car crashes that have been happening to his family and friends look a little different, don't they?"

"How do you mean?"

"Maybe those people knew a little too much. Or maybe they had money in the game and wanted out."

"I never thought of that," I admitted.

"Let's just hope"—again he glanced around furtively— "that nobody around here gets dragged into it."

"You mean Milton Babst? Or Bob Tedder?"

"Whoever."

With Martin on his way downtown to Staples I should have been able to concentrate on my work, but in my distracted state all I could think about was Jackie's murder and its aftermath. Since I woke up that morning I'd been agonizing over whether to take a copy of Eleanor's story down to the police station and give it to Detective Falcone. The story didn't prove anything; as evidence it was circumstantial at best. But it showed a motive, a means, an opportunity, and it might lead to the discovery of more solid proof. In my heart I knew I should turn it in. But then what would become of Eleanor? What would become of the writers' group?

I looked Sara up in my contacts list and dialed her office number. "Sara, it's me. Will Schaefer."

"Oh," she hesitated, surprised that I'd be calling her at work. "Hi."

"How are you?"

"OK, I guess. Still a little shaken up from last night."

"Yeah, I know. It's incredible, isn't it?"

"I still can't believe it."

"Sara," I said in a more confidential tone, "nobody wanted to say anything last night, but wasn't Eleanor's story a lot like what happened to Jackie?"

"A lot? No, I wouldn't say it was a lot like it."

"Well, the motive came across loud and clear."

"Plenty of people probably wanted to kill Jackie. Just about everybody, in fact."

"Yeah," I hesitated, "but not all of them followed her home from work with a sharp instrument in their purse."

"That's just a crazy coincidence. You're blowing it way out of proportion."

"It's really been bothering me," I insisted. "What do you think we should do?"

She sounded puzzled. "What do you mean?"

"Should we tell the police?"

"Tell them what?"

"I don't know. Tell them about the story. That detective—"

"What would you tell him?" she interrupted, a little tartly. "It's only a story."

"How do we know that's all it is?"

"What if it was one of your stories?"

"My stories aren't fantasies about murdering somebody."

"How do we know that? I've never been able to find any of your stories in print or on the internet."

"I publish under a different name."

She laughed. "That's a little suspicious, isn't it?"

I laughed a little too. "Okay, what are we going to do about Eleanor?"

There was a long silence, as if Sara was choosing her words carefully. "Will, I can't believe you'd even consider turning her into the cops for writing a story."

"That's not exactly—"

"It's a privacy issue, a free speech issue."

"A free speech issue?"

"The group is like a sanctuary where people have to feel free to express themselves. There's no evidence that Eleanor had anything to do with Jackie's death. We can't turn her in to the police just because of what she wrote in a story."

"I'm not talking about turning her in. Just wondering if we should tell the detective something he might need to know for his investigation."

"Is it an investigation or a witch hunt?"

The conversation continued in this vein for another ten minutes. Sara didn't mention how she felt about warrantless searches or ethnic profiling, but she was a diehard civil libertarian when it came to fiction writing. Nothing short of a full confession after a Miranda warning could have justified mentioning Eleanor's story to the police. Although I didn't agree with her logic, I came around to her point of view for less noble reasons. In one of our last and bitterest fights, Zelda had accused me of starting the writers' group for the sole purpose of meeting women—"You're a literary stalker," she claimed—and of course that wasn't true. But Sara had been irresistible from the moment I met her, and the current crisis gave me an excuse to draw her closer. Now that I knew how she felt about privacy and free speech, it was easy to put an end to my agonizing and give up the idea of disclosing Eleanor's story to Detective Falcone, at least for the time being. I know I'm not painting myself in a very flattering light when I admit this, but I think I deserve some credit for telling the truth on this point, now if not then, even if none of this matters anymore.

By the time I put down the phone, Sara and I had agreed that although Eleanor had the right to fantasize about the most gruesome crimes and record those fantasies in her stories without fear of being denounced to the police, we would keep our eyes open for any hard evidence that she had killed Jackie. If anything turned up, we would talk again and decide what to do. I was hoping—though I didn't say so— that my next meeting with Sara would be over coffee, if not over lunch or dinner. And as I trudged home that evening, I wondered what the other members of the group would think about these issues. Would they agree with Sara's enlightened, non-judgmental approach? Or would they opt for something more like the Salem witch trials?

I had my answer at the next meeting.

Sara's Journal
June 15

I can't believe Will wants to call the cops on Eleanor! He says write what you care about, let your imagination run wild—then when he hears what you write, his first instinct is to turn you in to the cops. I think I talked him out of it, which wasn't all that hard. He seems like a nice guy, but you've got to wonder if he's for real. Something fake about him, or maybe a little too nice for where my head is at these days. He's always flirting with me. I try to ignore him, try to pretend I'm so ethereal and self-absorbed I don't notice. Why do I do that? Is it just because of Carlos? Carlos (I think it was the night before I threw him out) said I play with men the way a cat plays with a mouse (don't all women do that a little?). He said men love me because I seem to have so little use for them. Oh, is that right, Carlos? I haven't met one of them yet that loved me, including you. Maybe I should be more like a dog, all bubbly and slobbery with plenty of panting and tail wagging. What would they call me then?

Mom didn't seem any worse today, I guess that's the best we can hope for. I've tried praying with her but I always end up in tears and that upsets her. Today Dad took off a couple of hours so I could go home and get some sleep.

Freddy of course has more important things to do than visit his dying mother.

I've got to get out of this funk. I used to be a happy person and I'm still capable of it. If only the temperature would drop about twenty degrees, maybe I could start breathing again. I can't even think of any jokes!

June 16

Aikido lessons going well. Shenzo says I'm the best student he's ever had. He thinks I'm almost ready to move up to the next level. What level is that? I ask him. I already have a black belt. He just lowers his eyes and says wait until the time is right.

Talked to Eleanor on the phone this evening. I feel so sorry for her because I know she didn't kill Jackie. She realizes that everybody thinks she did it but she doesn't want to act guilty or anything because that would just make it worse. She's a lot more upset about Jackie than worried about herself. Her husband is supporting her 100%.

In this heat it's hard to even know what you're doing. The TV news claims it's 99 degrees but I think it's much hotter than that.

6

Continuation by Will Schaefer

The weekend came and went, framed by languid mornings and long hazy evenings that tapered imperceptibly into night. Under these tropical conditions, time was not flying but oozing forward at an excruciating pace. I went out with some friends on Saturday night—yes, I do have friends—and found my way home well after midnight. When I awoke on Sunday morning I strolled down Eighth Avenue in my shorts and flip-flops, stopped for breakfast at a bagel shop just north of 14th street, and then wandered east on 14th Street. In Union Square Park—formerly devoted to rallying the starving masses, now to assuring a steady supply of gourmet foods to their descendants—I discovered one of the most extraordinary human beings I have ever met. He was a tall, elderly African-American with a shock of white hair that rose six inches above his forehead, topped by a red woolen stocking cap. Around his neck he wore a bandanna fashioned from an American flag, and over his bare chest a brace of red suspenders fastened to a pair of pin-striped trousers that extended just below his knees. He sat in a shady enclosure framed by a park bench, a garbage can and a couple of stunted trees, straddling an old black suitcase which housed all his worldly goods and also served as his place of business. Beside him stood a large cardboard carton, upended to the height of a table, on which were arrayed cans of shoe polish, some dirty rags, a shoe brush and an old laundry timer with a clock-like dial.

"Shine, sir?" he called out as I walked by.

I pointed to my flip-flops.

"How about a game of chess then?"

That made me stop. "Chess?"

"Thirty minutes to win, lose or draw." He pointed to the timer. "Checkmate costs the loser $20."

"Do you even have $20?"

"Not at the moment," he chuckled. "But I will, in about thirty minutes. Soon as I whup your ass."

I laughed and introduced myself.

"Dr. Gaston Gaylord de Goncourt," he replied with a bow. "Formerly of New Orleans, Louisiana. You can call me Dr. G."

Ah, a displaced Katrina victim, I thought. "I'd be glad to help you out."

That sparked a howl of derisive laughter. "Maybe you didn't hear what I said. I told you I'm a doctor, didn't I?" He leaned forward into the sunlight and showed me his deep-set eyes, mustard yellow and glimmering like a Siamese cat's. "That means I'm here to help you, not the other way around."

"How are you going to do that?"

"You look like maybe you're in some kind of trouble." He squinted like a physician examining a patient for signs of illness. "Something about a woman, maybe more than one woman."

I smiled, shrugged, took a step backwards. "It's not what you think."

"No"—he peered into my eyes and shook his head—"It's a lot worse. You're a worried man. A *very* worried man."

"It's not what you think," I repeated.

"What I think is, you need somebody to talk to."

"How much do you charge for that?"

His mouth opened in a long-toothed grin. "It's all included in the price of the chess game."

Before I could argue, Dr. G removed the shoeshine supplies from the top of his carton, revealing a hand-drawn chess board which he populated with mismatched pieces dumped out of a battered shoe box. He set the timer and the two of us were soon engrossed in a challenging game—I prided myself on my chess prowess—and as we played I found myself telling him about Jackie's death, Eleanor's story, Detective Falcone's investigation, and everything else that had been preying on my mind. I had to lower my voice to a whisper as spectators arrived—I assumed they were spectators—and sat in a row on the park bench: a middle-aged white guy who looked like a lawyer or accountant, a tall black teenager, a Hispanic hipster jabbering on his phone in Spanish. Dr. G bent toward me so he could hear what I told him, nodding and grunting occasionally but never taking his eyes off the board. A few minutes before the timer was set to go off, he pushed his queen forward and trapped my hapless king in a blind alley.

"Checkmate!"

He jumped up and danced around the table with his arms in the air. The spectators laughed, clapped, cheered him and jeered at me.

"OK," I conceded, peeling out a $20 bill. "That was a good warm-up. Now for the re-match."

"Not today," he admonished, wagging a bony finger in my face. "I got people waiting. You want a rematch, you got to make an appointment like everybody else."

He pulled a crumpled sheet of paper from his pocket and squinted as he held it up to the light. "Next available appointment is a week from today at 8:00 AM."

"Eight o'clock on Sunday morning? Couldn't we make it a little later? How about 11:00?"

"Sorry," he grinned. "The whole day's booked solid. You want the 8:00 o'clock slot or not?"

Sara's Journal
June 18

Mom was moved into hospice today. What does that mean?

She's in the same bed in the same room and they wheel her into the same dining room when it's time to eat. When I got there she was sitting across from Mr. Salvucci, a wizened little man who looks like a root that's been yanked out of the ground.

It means they're just going to let you die, Mr. Salvucci says. Apparently he's in hospice too.

They have no treatments for cancer, he says. Only experimental drugs the doctors get paid for testing on you as their guinea pig. That's the most you can hope for, to be a guinea pig in a clinical trial. If the drug works, it's approved by the FDA and it's not an experimental drug anymore and they won't get paid for using it. That's why we're in hospice. We've had too many treatments to make it into the next generation of guinea pigs.

Mom pushes her food away and I wheel her down to the lounge where family members can visit with their loved ones. Loving your Mom is supposed to be a natural law, like gravity. She's calm and peaceful now, even funny at times, but in her prime she was usually angry, not warm and loving like most mothers. And now that she is helpless she's a sweet little old lady and it's me who's cold and selfish and can never do enough for her.

Continuation by Will Schaefer

An hour or two after sunset on Sunday night I glided down the stairs in hopes of finding a breeze and as I stepped outside I felt the eerie presence of Wolfgang in the misty twilight. He was not growling but silently giving me the evil eye, with his mistress, recognizable by her pale face and spiky orange hair, manipulating his leash with both hands like a puppeteer. From her wrist dangled a plastic bag full of dog turds, a token of Wolfgang's efforts to add nutrients to the environment. She sometimes called him the Silver Ghost and that was exactly how he looked in the shadowy half-light, judging me mutely and curiously as the dead judge the living.

Zelda was the first to speak, breaking the spell with a laugh. "I got your ridiculous note," she said.

"What was ridiculous about it?"

"That you think I'd go to the trouble of waking up in the middle of the night to harass you with crank calls."

"It sounds like something you'd do."

"If it was me, I wouldn't hang up when you answered. I'd make death threats."

Wolfgang growled his assent. "If I were you," I said, laughing foolishly, "I'd be more worried about receiving death threats than handing them out."

Wolfgang growled again, straining at his leash. "What's that supposed to mean?" Zelda demanded.

"You're a friend of Paul Gratzky's, aren't you? Haven't you heard what's been happening to all his friends?"

She hesitated. "I'm only his… ex-friend."

"So much the worse." I don't know why I said that but the effect was electrifying. She stumbled forward, barely restraining the dog from pulling himself within striking distance. I took a step back.

"What have you heard?" she demanded.

"Nothing, really. Just a rumor."

"What rumor?"

"That maybe all those accidents that have happened to Gratzky's family and friends weren't really accidents. That maybe all those people had to die because they knew too much."

"That's ridiculous," she said defiantly. "Who did you hear that from?"

"Never mind who I heard it from."

"You're probably lying about this just like you lie about everything else. No, I take that back. It's more creative than anything you could come up with. You must have copied it out of a book."

She tightened the leash and allowed the dog to pull her forward. "Now please get out of the way. Unless you want to be eaten alive."

I took the threat seriously and stepped aside to let them pass. Wolfgang, to his credit, gave no sign of wanting to devour me, but wished me a long goodbye with his hollow, soulless eyes.

Sara's Journal
June 19

Got to get back to writing. Maybe that will cheer me up.

Idea for a story: a woman named Nika who cuts hair at Celeste's Unisex in Tribeca. Men are fascinated by her, probably because she has so little interest in them. She knows that love is an illusion. She cares only about herself, but men, possibly for that reason, find her irresistible. They want her to love them as much as she loves herself.

The shop is owned by Celeste, a 48-year-old divorcee with three teenage sons. Celeste has a rule: No flirting with, or by, customers; no dating or sex with customers. I'm not running a massage parlor, she likes to say. Nevertheless, she calls the haircutters "the girls" like whores in a brothel. Nika likes the other haircutters well enough except for Mary Ann, her best friend. Mary Ann, a 37-year-old redhead, never married, stands beside her all day dishing out stupid advice. Hers is a world of dangers and outrages which can be avoided through the simple expedient of being a loser. You can be a loser too, she seems to be telling Nika. Just follow my example and you'll be spared the depravities of men. Innocent Nika. If Mary Ann only knew.

This isn't cheering me up. If it wasn't so freaking hot I'd go to the aikido academy and work out. If the heat gets any worse I won't be responsible for my actions!

June 20

More on the story:

One of Nika's regulars at Celeste's Unisex is Mario Migliori, a well-known artist. A quiet, brooding man who always gives her a big tip. He's in his mid-fifties and his hair is an embarrassing mane of gray starting about three inches below the crown and drooping down to his shoulders. He comes in for a trim every week and seems to enjoy the sensation of Nika hovering over him, her fingers brushing against his neck. Last week, with a wink and a comical smile, he pressed a $50 bill into her hand after he paid Celeste. Mary Ann, the loser who cuts hair next to Nika, must have reported this to Celeste. Now as he steps through the door Celeste takes him aside and gives him a warning. A joke, he thinks, but no, it isn't a joke. When he gives Nika another fifty, this time with a peck on the cheek, Celeste swoops in and bans him from the shop.

I'm not running a massage parlor, she tells him. You'll have to get your kicks somewhere else.

One night about eleven o'clock Nika is returning from her aikido class in the drizzling rain. She walks past the Pergamon Gallery on Franklin Street where Mario Migliori is about to open a one-artist show. She peeks through the window and sees nothing but bare walls and a few strips of electrical tape dangling from the ceiling. Then she spots Mario on the floor, peering up critically at the electrical tape. When he notices Nika he lurches toward her on his hands and knees, laughing and smiling, until his face is pressed against the window in a funhouse grin. She backs away, embarrassed and ashamed, as if she's been caught peeping into the monkey house after the zoo is closed.

Later, when she reads a review of the opening, she realizes that those strips of electrical tape are all there is to the show.

Do I dare read this to the group? Is Will going to recognize himself with an Italian name, gray hair, an artist instead of a writer? I doubt if he'll notice the resemblance. What about Kate? Does she know what a loser she is?

7

Continuation by Will Schaefer

On Tuesday night I served iced tea instead of coffee and we all stood around talking about Jackie: how shocked we were by her death, how much we would miss her, how sad it must be for Larry and the rest of her family. Eleanor was the last to arrive, shuffling bashfully into the apartment laden with the fruits of a long afternoon shopping in SoHo. Everyone lowered their voices to a murmur and the conversation trailed off into an awkward silence. It was as if a bereaved member of Jackie's family had entered the room, bringing the same atmosphere of awe that you feel at a funeral, and the same kind of superstitious embarrassment, the embarrassment of being alive when someone else is dead. The grim reaper must be consoled with tears and obsequies lest you fall victim to his whims—that's what funerals are all about, and this was as close to a funeral for Jackie as we were going to get. Eleanor was her usual timid self, of course, but it was hard not to view her self-effacement in a new light.

Before Eleanor's arrival, the group had divided into two factions: Brian, Josh and myself, who wanted to confront her with our suspicions, and Sara and Kate, who seemed determined to reassure and protect her. Brian, the security expert, advocated giving Eleanor's story to the police, and in this he was seconded by Josh, who ventured the opinion, based on his experience in the insurance industry, that in the long run everyone gets what they deserve. The women took a more sympathetic approach, and I played the mediator. "Don't we owe it to Eleanor," I suggested, "to at least confront her with our suspicions and give her a chance to defend herself before we go to the police?" Kate nodded and Sara gave me an approving smile. Josh shook his head gravely. Brian, for reasons that would soon become apparent, laughed out loud and turned away.

After Eleanor arrived and everyone had taken their seats—no one dared to sit in the director's chair that Jackie had claimed as her own—I suggested that we observe a moment of silence, after which we could all share our remembrances and thoughts about Jackie. We lowered our eyes and concentrated on our own thoughts—in my case wondering how long a "moment" should be in such a situation—and after a long interval it was Brian who broke the spell.

"That may be the only moment of silence Jackie ever had," he smiled.

Kate shot him a disapproving glance but the rest of us laughed. Sara and I both offered some eulogistic remarks, but it soon became clear that apart from shock and sympathy at her demise no one was overly disappointed that Jackie would be absent from the group. Eleanor listened intently, nodding and smiling as if our remarks were intended to comfort her.

It was Brian's turn to read that night. In defiance of the weather he was wearing a suit and tie, as he often did when coming to meetings directly from work. Beads of sweat glistened on his forehead and his glasses seemed to be slipping down his nose. When the discussion about Jackie ran its course he pulled a neatly folded handkerchief from his breast pocket and daubed the sweat off his brow and his glasses.

Then, without any introduction, he pulled a typed manuscript from his briefcase and began to read in the cocky, streetwise voice of Detective Val Osbourne: *"'I'm in homicide.' I like to say that, especially to white people who don't know I'm a cop. They think I'm just stating my line of work, like 'I'm in real estate' or 'I'm in construction.' If they stare back in disbelief, it's not at my occupation but at my use of a three-syllable word."* Val Osbourne is an undercover cop who enjoys masquerading as a wealthy rap star and tweaking the high-society types who try to hit him up for contributions—like the kindly Mrs. Engelbert who is the organizer of a gala for the Schweitzer Hospital Center. His current investigation has him working overtime: a Dominican kid named Selwyn Fernandez has confessed, on videotape, to stabbing a white legal secretary named Christine Wenzel with a pair of scissors in her home in the Bronx. And now his attorney, an overzealous, overbearing Legal Aid lawyer named Bridget Leary (with a sinking feeling I recognized her as Kate on steroids), claims the confession was coerced. Val despises Bridget Leary but suspects that the Fernandez kid is innocent. The kid says he saw another woman—an "old lady," he calls her—leaving the house in a hurry. Val sets out to find that woman so Selwyn Fernandez can be saved.

The story unfolded like a TV cop show and is hardly worth retelling. But it included some memorable characters. There was the victim, Christine Wenzel, enjoying an illicit affair with an attorney in her office. Her husband Larry, a high school math teacher who can't take his eyes off the Mets game even while Val questions him about his wife's murder. Steve Engelbert, the nerdy Trusts and Estates partner she's sleeping with, and his twenty-something daughter, "a little bullied and a little bored, as if she'd spent too much of her life doing all the things you're supposed to do to get into a good school" (a shiver flashed through the room when Val described her as having "a flat chest and a big attitude"). And then of course there was Mrs. Engelbert, the kindly East Side matron—obviously modeled on Eleanor—who, under Val's questioning, blurted out just enough to incriminate herself for premeditated murder.

The group seemed ready to boil over by the time Brian had finished reading. Kate clawed at her notebook and made chewing motions with her mouth. Sara gazed around the room like a frightened deer. Josh, who had sunk lower and lower in his chair as the story went on, seemed ready to burst out of his skin. And what about Eleanor, who in the story had just pleaded guilty to first-degree murder? She was the only one who kept her cool. She smiled sweetly when Brian finished and told him in her quiet way how much she'd enjoyed the story. Either she'd missed the whole point—in which case she must have been innocent—or she was a cunning psychopath deflecting our suspicions with a Big Lie. If it was strategy, it succeeded brilliantly. None of us dared mention what was in plain view: that Brian had brought Eleanor's story of the previous week to its logical conclusion and in the process convicted her of murdering Jackie.

Instead we focused on technique. "I liked the way Val Osbourne told his tale," I said cautiously. "Especially at the beginning. Toward the end his voice seemed less idiosyncratic and authentic."

"That's a fair point," Brian agreed.

"Although at times I found myself wondering if the shift in voice represented a basic tension in Val Osbourne's character. Is he really a street punk turned cop, as he likes to portray himself? Or is he a middle class kid pretending to be a street punk turned cop?"

Brian lowered his eyes in embarrassment and I had my answer.

Kate stopped chewing and started growling. "I didn't like the 'flat chest and a big attitude.'"

"I could take that out," he said evenly, "but that wouldn't be Val Osbourne talking. That would be me."

"So he's a pig and you're not? Is that it?"

He grimaced. "Something like that."

"Frankly, I doubt if your attitude is any different from your sicko character's. You're the one who thought him up."

"OK, time out!" I interrupted. The subtext of this debate, as we all knew, was not simply Val Osbourne's macho attitudes but his portrayal of Bridget Leary, the defense attorney, as a grotesque caricature of Kate. I needed to get the discussion back on a literary level. "The trouble with your argument," I told Kate, "is that it proves too much. A writer has to be able to create characters that are less moral, less likeable than himself, even if they're shameful or repulsive. You can't attribute the characters' qualities or beliefs to the writer."

"But if he presents this creep as a hero, then he ought to be held responsible."

"Especially"—it was the first time Sara had spoken—"if the women he's writing about are sitting right in front of him." She turned her penetrating gaze on Brian. "That's my chest you're talking about. Is it too flat for your liking?"

"This is ridiculous!" Brian exploded. "You're focusing on a couple of words about a minor character."

"That's right," Sara pursued. "A very minor character. Why is Mrs. Engelbert's daughter even in the story? Just to give you a chance to talk about my breasts and your bigoted views on where I went to college?"

Josh cleared his throat, and since he so rarely spoke we all turned to face him. In his black suit he looked like an old-time magician, brooding, profound, judgmental. When he spoke he tilted his dark brow forward, so that the whites of his eyes sunk to the bottom. "This is wrong," he said in a low, almost liturgical voice. "We should remember what the story is about."

"And what is it about, in your opinion?" Kate demanded.

Slowly, he waved both hands in front of him, palms outward, as if trying to describe some hideous shape. "The punishment of an adulteress. An adulteress who could be no one other than Jackie."

"You mean the characters in Jackie's stories," I corrected him.

Kate ignored my efforts to keep the discussion on a literary level and turned back to Brian. "I think it's disgusting that you would use a story like this to settle a score with a dead woman."

"What do you mean 'settle a score?'" Brian pressed her.

"Because of the way she depicted the black security guard in her last story. You were really angry about that and you let her know it. And now she's dead and you can't let go of it."

"You weren't too happy about the way she depicted you, as I recall."

"No, but I didn't kill her off because of it."

"You think I killed her?"

"In your story you did."

Eleanor had sat quietly through these attacks on Brian, and now, astonishingly, she rose to his defense. "Kate," she said softly, "I understand why you're upset about Brian's characterization of Jackie. Speak no ill of the dead, and all that. But don't you see, if anyone is upset it should be me. The whole point of the story is to accuse me of murdering Jackie. And I can't really blame Brian, based on my story about Margaret that I read for the group last week. Margaret had every reason in the world to kill the other woman, and so did Mrs. Engelbert in Brian's story. If I were Margaret or Mrs. Engelbert and another woman was trying to steal my husband, that's exactly what I would have done."

"Did you kill her then?"

"Kill whom?"

"Jackie?"

"No, of course not." She smiled back at Kate as if she were humoring a lunatic. "You mean in reality? Certainly not. Howard and I were up at our Vermont house the day she was killed."

"You were?"

"Of course. In the summer we're up there every week from Wednesday through Sunday. I explained that to Detective Falcone."

That was the last meeting Brian ever attended. By the time we adjourned everyone was exhausted by the atmosphere of tension and hostility that seemed to be poisoning the group. The discussion had dissolved into a series of long silences, made excruciating by the effort to avoid further offense. We were all relieved when it was over. Kate gathered her things and left without saying goodbye, followed by Josh, who seemed anxious to keep up with her. Sara idled by the door as if to give them a head start and then slipped out with a quick, troubled glance in my direction. Eleanor, ironically, seemed least affected by the emotions she had unleashed. I remember thinking at the time how kind and thoughtful she was to approach Brian as the others fled, reassuring him in her quiet way that she had taken no offense at his story.

The downstairs buzzer rang. It was Howard, Eleanor's fawning Oliver Hardy of a husband—presumably coveted by every woman on the planet—who in obedience to her phone summons had rushed over in a cab to escort her home. That left me alone with Brian. In a one-on-one situation he was more relaxed, less defensive, less inclined to seek refuge in aloofness or sarcasm. "I didn't expect my story to elicit so much hostility," he smiled.

I raised my eyebrows. "You didn't?"

"Well, maybe just a little."

We shared a laugh. "Great characterizations, even if some of them may have hit a little too close to home for this audience."

"Eleanor has nothing to fear from me," he said.

"Or from anyone. It sounds like she has a pretty good alibi."

I assumed he'd stayed behind for a reason but apparently he just wanted to chat. We talked about his writing and his job and his kids—a boy and a girl he was working overtime to send to a private elementary school so they wouldn't end up like Selwyn Fernandez in his story. I got the impression that their mother, who had custody except on weekends, wasn't much help, though he was too much of a gentleman to say why. His writing was important to him, but his kids were what he really cared about and he seemed grateful for the opportunity to tell me about them. After about ten minutes he started inching toward the door. "Well, I'd better get going," he said. "It's been a tough week."

"It's only Tuesday," I pointed out.

"One of my co-workers was killed last night in a hit-and-run accident right outside our building. A guy I worked with every day."

"I'm really sorry to hear that." Then it struck me that I might have known the victim. "Was it anybody who worked on the project in my building?"

"He might have. Alan Stone. African-American, about my age. He was one of the technicians."

"I think I remember him."

Brian turned around in the doorway and smiled good-bye. "I'd better go."

"You look like you could use some rest," I said, offering a limp handshake. I was pretty tired myself.

"Yeah, I haven't been able to get much sleep lately. The phone keeps waking me up in the middle of the night."

Suddenly I was wide awake. "Your phone rings in the night? You cell phone?"

"No, my land line. I don't know why I still have it anymore. All I get are crank calls."

"How many times does it ring?"

My question startled him. "Why do you ask? It always rings twice, unless I pick it up before it stops ringing."

"Then what happens?"

"If I answer it, it just goes dead."

8

The morning after Brian read his story, I sat at my desk pretending to review a press release as I agonized over the events of the past two weeks. Evidently my distraction was obvious. "Another bad night with the writers' group?" Martin asked as he brought in my morning mail.

"Yes," I acknowledged. "The atmosphere has turned toxic since Jackie died."

"Murder will do that," he said. "It's not good for morale. Although a little selective weeding of the population in this office would do wonders for *my* morale."

He was referring to Helen, who (as he explained in detail) had already slighted him several times that morning. In my agitated state I couldn't bear to listen to any more of his complaints. "Your morale is important to me," I said earnestly. "I've got an idea. Why don't you take the rest of the day off?"

"If you don't need anything."

"No, I'll be fine."

"Okay," he conceded. "If you insist. I've got some photocopying to do and then I'll get out of your hair. By the way"—he leaned forward with an air of triumph—"did you see this morning's *Times*? It's just as I predicted. They're saying Gratzky was responsible for all those so-called random deaths."

"That's ridiculous. His wife died of cancer, his mother and father were killed on the same day in two separate plane crashes—"

"The evidence is circumstantial, as it almost always is. But according to the prosecutor, Gratzky's guilt can be proven statistically using the same mathematical models he uses to run his hedge fund."

That made me laugh. "The prosecutor says the hedge fund is a fraud. If those models work for one thing—"

But Martin was already running out the door.

With Martin out of the way I decided to call Sara and see if she could help me sort things out. "I can't talk now," she said when I finally negotiated my way through the voicemail labyrinth and reached her on the phone.

"Could you meet me at lunchtime? Grab a sandwich and go for a walk? I need to talk to you."

We met on the steps of the New York Public Library. She was friendly but not warm, enigmatic as always and exceptionally beautiful in the moist breeze that was tantalizing the city that afternoon. It was 89 degrees—the first day under 90 in two weeks—and people seemed incredulous, disoriented, almost ready to take their woolens out of storage.

"At least the temperature has come down to the level where an earthling can survive for an hour or two," I said.

"Let's go for a walk."

We walked around a few blocks and ended back in Bryant Park, just behind the Library, where we found a vendor selling Middle Eastern food. He sold us a couple of gyros and we sat down on a bench next to another vendor who was roasting chestnuts on a small brazier.

"I'm worried about the way things are going with the group," I said, biting into my sandwich. "It's starting to seem more like an encounter group than a creative experience."

"Jackie started all that."

"I know. But now that Jackie's gone it seems to get worse every week."

She flicked a strand of dark hair away from her eyes. "I didn't like that story Brian read."

"Nobody did. Though actually I—"

"He shouldn't be allowed to bring in material like that."

"Shouldn't be allowed?" I could hardly believe what I was hearing. "What happened to free speech and all that?"

"Free speech doesn't mean you can go around insulting everybody."

"Of course it does."

She smiled her mischievous smile. "All I mean is that two can play that game. When it's my turn I'm going to get him back."

I would have thrown up my hands but by this time they were covered with small fragments of my gyro sandwich. "That's what I'm talking about!" I protested. "This isn't what's supposed to be going on in a writers' group. I'm a writer, not a psychiatrist."

"We don't need a psychiatrist."

"I'm not so sure about that. But I know I don't have the qualifications for the job."

We ate in silence for a few minutes, aware that any further discussion might be dangerous to our relationship. At least that's what I thought, having no idea what Sara thought of our relationship or even whether she thought we had one.

"Who eats those things?" she finally asked.

"What things?"

"Those roasted chestnuts. I've lived in New York all my life and I've never seen anyone eating them."

"I thought you grew up in New Jersey."

"All right," she laughed. "I was exaggerating. Actually I was born in Santiago, Chile. Did you know that?"

"Yes, I think I did. Your father's a doctor, isn't he?"

"A surgeon," she nodded. "And one of the best, if you take his word for it."

I liked where the conversation was going. Exchanging family lore is an important step in building a relationship. "Do you come from a large family?"

"Two sisters and a brother. I'm the oldest. How about you?"

"I'm the oldest of five kids. The others are all rednecks now so we don't have much in common. I grew up in a small town in Missouri, right on the Mississippi River."

"Just like Mark Twain," she said. "That must be why you became a writer."

"I don't know. I certainly didn't have the kind of idyllic boyhood Mark Twain wrote about, except for having an abusive drunk for a father. We were about as poor as Job's turkeys, as my grandmother used to say."

"Somehow you got out of there."

"Yeah. I left home when I was seventeen and a couple years later I talked my way into a writing program at the University of Houston."

I could practically feel Sara warming up to me. "How did you get to New York?" she asked.

"Well, that took a while. To get through school I worked at every job you could imagine, plus a few you probably wouldn't want to hear about. I was lucky enough to get a couple of stories published, and after I got my degree I found a teaching job at a small local college. The money wasn't really enough to live on and I was ready to throw in the towel and start selling life insurance. Then one of my friends was driving up to New York and I came along for the ride." I didn't mention that the friend in question was my then-girlfriend Lauren, with whom I lived for five years. "Before I knew it I'd landed a job as a public relations writer at Zunax Corporation. The perfect day job that doesn't interfere too much with my writing."

"How did you happen to start the group?"

"Oh, that grew out of a course I taught at the Y. It's just something I like to do."

"It must be a great way to meet people."

"It's a great way to meet interesting people," I agreed. "You can meet boring people anywhere."

She looked down at her watch. "I've got to get back."

We parted where we had met, in front of the library steps. "I wouldn't worry about the group too much," she reassured me. "Things will get back to normal."

"I hope you're right."

"We're like a family. We have our ups and downs, and some of us have our issues. But basically we enjoy each other or we wouldn't be there. It'll work out all right." She started to walk away but stopped and turned back around. "By the way, who's reading next week?"

"Well, Brian read last night, and the week before it was Eleanor."

"So next week?"

"Next week would be Kate."

Sara's Journal
June 22

Last night I couldn't write anything, I was so upset about Brian's story, and then this afternoon talking to Will wasn't much better. What's the matter with these guys? Do they think women were put on this planet for their amusement? I suspect it was the other way around, and it's not working out. We are not amused.

Why isn't your father here? Mom asks me. I tell her I don't know, I haven't talked to him today. I hope Freddy can come, she says. I always love to see Freddy.

Saint Freddy. Five years out of school and still no sign of any ambition beyond hanging out in bars with his friends. He makes an appearance every couple of weeks for about fifteen minutes but Mom talks about him endlessly, as if selfish Sara, with her daily visits and sleepless nights, could never hope to match Freddy in his generosity and compassion.

June 23

Carlos keeps leaving messages as if I'd want to talk to him. He's trying to pull me back into his violent, drugged out world—like I didn't learn my lesson. He used to make fun of my writing because he saw it as a threat, my ticket out of his nightmare. After I joined the group he warned me not to write about him. No chance of that! The group seemed like my salvation at first but it went downhill after Jackie joined. I know I shouldn't say this, but it's a whole lot better without her. I'm not the only one who feels that way, and it's not just about Jackie. Brian and Kate ought to get together and fight it out like a couple of pit bulls. Sometimes I wish Eleanor and I could just go on without the others—she's the Mom I never had (I shouldn't say that either). With the whole group listening I can't write about my actual life, only some fake life I never lived. I feel like they're spying on me, judging me (in Will's case getting ready to call the cops). As a result all my stories are impersonations, which is a shame. Will says I'm the most talented writer in the group. I like him and he likes me, but he doesn't seem to realize I'm a work of fiction. It's like the Ray Charles song: *You Don't Know Me.*

June 24

Message on the answering machine from Dad. Says he has to work late and can't come to the nursing home until nine. On the way from aikido class to the bus I duck into a bodega about twenty blocks from where he works. And there he is buying a six pack; he seems disconcerted to see me. Then an Asian woman, not much over 40, sidles up next to him with an avocado in her hand and asks him whether he feels like having guacamole. He mumbles our names—her name is Stephanie—and we exchange looks, one woman to another. It's obvious that Stephanie and Dad are sleeping together. Do you live around here? I ask her. Yeah. Just around the corner.

Later, at the nursing home, I confront him in the reception area. I expect him to be embarrassed but he's not. When we were growing up he worked long hours to support the family but he never complained. Because he loves us—that's what Mom said when I asked her why he was never home. Because he loves us.

Now he sits in front of me, leaning forward in his chair, keeping his voice down so the receptionist won't hear what he's saying. It's time to have a talk, he says. About your Mom.

They put her in hospice. I guess that means she's dying.

That's what it means, he agrees. And that's why we need to talk, before she becomes a saint.

I understand what he means. Any dead person can become a saint if they confess and repent their sins before they die. Mom will be careful to repent at the last possible moment.

I never should have married her, he goes on. She has a bad temper, a violent temper, you can't imagine. Her sister tried to tell me about it before we got married but I didn't understand what she was trying to tell me. After we were married I began to understand but I thought it was something that would pass, something I could help her with. Then you were born and I had a lot on my mind. By the time Freddy came along I realized that the marriage was a failure. Worse than a failure. A mistake.

Why did you stay together?

I thought about divorcing her. But I decided against it, for the family's sake.

The family's sake? You mean me?

You and your brother.

Freddy could have grown up under a rock and he'd be exactly the same as he is now.

For your sake, then. I stayed with her for your sake. I thought you needed a mother.

It's going to take me a while to absorb this. He admitted it's been going on for years with one woman or another. Why didn't I ever suspect anything? No wonder Mom was mad all the time. But it's OK. He did it for my sake.

9

Continuation by *Will Schaefer*

On Sunday morning, while saner men were having breakfast
in bed, going to church or sleeping off a drunk, I sat on an
empty crate on the edge of Union Square Park watching
knights and bishops and queens contend on a hand-drawn
chessboard as I told a homeless witch doctor in red
suspenders everything that happened to me during the past
week. Why am I doing this? I asked myself. Most people in
New York have a psychiatrist, which I can't afford—instead I
have Dr. G: I tell him everything. That morning I told him
about Zelda, Sara, Brian, the phone calls. I told him about
my job, Martin, Bob Tedder, Paul Gratzky. And why did I
confide all this to a stranger? Because Dr. G had no
connection to my world and never would. And unlike most
of the people I knew, I could trust him.

"I can't figure out this writer group of yours," he said that
morning, about twenty minutes into our game. "Nobody
seems to like anybody else. Instead they kill each other off
like dogs and still come back for more."

"Sounds like you and me," I observed, keeping an eye on
his queen.

"We're at least honest with each other." He ignored the
queen and instead moved one of his bishops forward,
opening a diagonal attack on my king. "You can't believe a

word these folks say. When they ain't out killing each other, they're dreaming up a new pack of lies, which they write down and read out loud to the group."

"It's fiction," I objected. "Not lies."

"How can you tell the difference?"

"It's only a lie if you expect somebody to believe it."

He showed me his long-toothed grin. "What if it's true and you're hoping they *don't* believe it? What is it then?"

That was a good question, which I'd never asked myself before. I jumped one of my horses in front of his bishop to block its path to my king.

"You see," he laughed, waving his hand over the board like a magician, "that's what make chess such a interesting game. It's all there in plain view—the problem, the solution, everything you need to know. But you never see what's coming 'til it's too late."

He reached down and nudged a pawn forward—one of his most insignificant pawns, which I'd ignored until then, and which I promptly captured with one of my own. His queen stole in to nab my pawn, revealing a well-planned, coordinated line of attack that left my king no chance of escape.

"Checkmate."

The timer went off, signaling that it was only by grace that the game had gone on as long as it did. I started to mumble some face-saving excuse, but Dr. G cut me off.

"That be $20, please," he smiled. "Whatever's on your mind, we can talk about it next week."

Sara's Journal
June 26

Met Freddy at one of his hangouts in the West Village to break the news. Not that Mom is dying—he already knew that—but that Dad has hated her all his life and wishes he'd divorced her long ago.

Why didn't he? Freddy asks, sipping his Irish coffee.

For our sake. Can you believe that? Apparently he thought it would do us good to spend our childhood in a horror movie.

Hey, it wasn't exactly a horror movie.

I'm trying to suppress the anger that's been welling up inside me since Dad's revelations. Anger toward Mom for her lifelong meanness, toward Dad for condoning it. And now toward Freddy for going through life without noticing or being affected by anything.

Don't you remember the time she came after me with the butcher knife?

Freddy's forehead wrinkles under the unaccustomed stress of deep thought. In the kitchen one time?

It started in the kitchen. She was yelling at me about something while she carved some meat with a butcher knife and when I talked back she came after me with the knife. I ran away and she chased me all over the apartment with it. I had to barricade myself in my room to keep her from slashing me.

Freddy ventures a weak smile. That's not how I remember it, exactly. But whatever.

What do you mean, whatever?

He sets his coffee down and leans forward, flicking a loose strand of hair behind his ear. OK, she could be mean. Nasty sometimes. Threatening but never actually violent that I remember. But whatever happened then, that was then. Now she's a shriveled up old lady dying of cancer.

I signal to the waiter, avoiding Freddy's eyes. I don't know if I'm going to care or not when she dies.

Listen, this is your last chance to forgive her.

Forgive her? Why should I forgive her?

For your own sake, if you can't think of any other reason. This is your last chance.

The waiter brings the check and I reach in my purse for a $20 bill. Freddy makes no move to contribute, offering another one of his pearls of wisdom instead.

If you don't forgive her now, he says, you'll have to live with your bitterness for the rest of your life.

I snap my purse shut and lay the $20 bill on the table.

It's a small price to pay, I tell him.

Continuation by Will Schaefer

People seemed a little wary of each other as they arrived at the next meeting. Eleanor came up first and smiled shyly at the others as they drifted into the apartment and found their usual seats. In the kitchen, where I manned the buzzer to open the downstairs door, I mixed up some cold lemonade and watched for Sara's arrival out of the corner of my eye. She barely glanced in my direction but said a few words to Eleanor, then sat down and buried her nose in her laptop. After a moment there was another buzz and the hulking figure of Josh appeared in the doorway. He strode into the room like a magician in his dark suit, waving a large handkerchief which he used, as soon as he had taken his seat on the couch, to swab the sweat from his forehead.

Kate made her entrance after everyone else had sat down, as usual in a rumpled T-shirt and jeans. She was an attractive woman in spite of her unflattering clothes, with shoulder-length red hair and fair, freckled skin that seemed to be getting a little blotchy as the summer wore on. Since it was her night to read, she tried to break the ice with some friendly chatter, but the others seemed unresponsive, smiling and then turning away as if they were embarrassed to be there. She was excited in a way I'd never seen her before. She kept talking and laughing as she pulled out her manuscript and handed out copies to the others. Then for the first time she seemed to notice that one member of the group was missing.

"Where's Brian?" she asked, as if any of us would know.

"He probably had to work late," Eleanor suggested.

"There was a fire on one of the subways tonight," said Josh.

"Really?" Kate gasped. "I hope he's all right. Let's give him a couple more minutes at least."

She continued with her chatter for another few minutes and when Brian still failed to appear I said there was something I wanted to bring up. "Not to alarm anyone," I said, "but have any of you been getting anonymous phone calls in the middle of the night?"

Kate's excitement clenched into suspicion and she turned on me with an accusatory stare. "What do you know about that?"

"All I know," I said evenly, "is that I've been getting anonymous calls, usually between midnight and three in the morning, and so has Brian."

"He would say that," she said.

"What do you mean?"

"If he was making the calls, he would claim he was getting them, wouldn't he?"

I tried to stay calm. "Is there any reason to think it's Brian who's been making the calls? Have you talked to him?"

"No," she admitted. "He—well, whoever it is—always hangs up before I can answer."

"Maybe you ought to talk to your friend Zelda," I said. "If you ask me, she's the number one suspect."

"No," Kate frowned. "A woman wouldn't do that." She glanced toward Sara and Eleanor for female support. "I've had the feeling lately that I was being stalked. Has anyone else had that feeling?"

Sara and Eleanor both shook their heads, and Kate turned her accusatory eyes back toward me. "Don't ask me why I feel that way. Women get raped and murdered every day who had that feeling and couldn't explain why."

"Has anyone else been getting these calls?" I asked.

"My only phone is my cell phone," Josh said, "and I turn it off at night."

"Same here," said Sara.

We all looked at Eleanor. "We still have a house phone, of course," she said cautiously. "If it rang in the middle of the night I assume Howard would answer it. He hasn't mentioned anything about anonymous calls."

"How many times does it ring?" I asked Kate.

"Usually twice," she said. "Only last night it rang three times."

"Three times? Are you sure?"

"Of course I'm sure. How many times did yours ring last night?"

"I had it turned off," I said. "I can't stand being woken up by it."

Since Brian was so late, I suggested that Kate go ahead and start her reading without him.

"I hope he's all right," she said. She seemed genuinely concerned, but after what she'd said about the phone calls I wondered if she had a hidden agenda. The previous week Brian had read a story that offended all the women in the group, especially Kate, who was portrayed as a shrewish, unethical defense lawyer. Would her story be an instrument of revenge?

At last, when I had handed out all the cold lemonade I could make and we could put it off no longer, Kate began to read: *"I met Maria Reyes three years ago when she came to the shelter for the first time.* She had a bullied, distrustful look in her eyes, bruises and cuts on her face and cigarette burns on her legs. Her speech—she spoke only Spanish—was halting, and there

were times when she just gazed around avoiding eye contact."
Gradually Maria Reyes told her story to the narrator, a social
worker at the women's shelter. It was a nauseating tale of
poverty, rape and abuse, beginning in Honduras and
proceeding to Mexico, which she passed through on a hellish
freight train under the 'protection' of a *coyote* who killed her
boyfriend and took her as his whore. When the *coyote* was
arrested she ended up in Juarez with a pimp named Ernesto,
from whom she stole some money and escaped to New York.
In New York she found a housecleaning job for a wealthy
family on the East Side named Gamael, a doctor's wife and
daughter who treated her like a slave. The daughter had
acquired an expensive education and had nothing but
contempt for a young woman who lacked her advantages. In
spite of her misfortunes Maria seemed a very sweet person.
Thin and delicate, with beautiful skin and straight black hair,
she had an inner glow, an air of innocence, that shone
through even when her face was bruised and swollen—even
when she was getting ready to kill someone.

That moment came when Ernesto tracked her down in
New York. He beat and tortured her and for a few days she
found refuge at the shelter. About a week later the social
worker received a call from a Detective Orly, who was
investigating the bludgeoning death of a man named Ernesto
Benitez. Detective Orly seemed like an unlikely cop, the
social worker thought, with a high forehead and a pair of
rimless glasses, more like what you'd expect in an English
professor. But as it turned out, his interest in Maria was far
from academic. A month later she came back to the shelter,
bruised and badly shaken. It wasn't Ernesto this time, she
said—it was her new boyfriend, Bill. A real sicko, even more
of a creep than Ernesto. Their relationship consisted entirely

of coercive sex, and if Bill didn't get exactly what he wanted
he became furiously impotent.

The social worker who is relating this story has heard
about Detective William Orly. It seems he met the same fate
as Ernesto Benitez—dead in an alley, his head smashed from
behind, stab wounds all over his body. And what's become
of Maria? She had that inner glow, that aura of innocence
that made you think she'd put up with anything. No one
thought she had it in her to fight back, or even to run away.
But she's disappeared and the police will never find her. *"Is
that all you'll need from me?"* the social worker asks. *"I've told you
everything I know. If you want to have this typed up, I'll wait. Or I
can come back and sign it tomorrow."*

I think the only positive emotion anyone felt after hearing
Kate's story was relief that it was over. After an awkward
silence I ventured a compliment. "I loved the twist at the
end," I said. "That the whole story was a statement being
given to the police. I didn't see that coming."

"That wasn't the only twist," Kate retorted.

No one followed up on that point. Instead there was
another long silence.

"It's hard for me to relate to fantasy," Eleanor murmured,
shifting in her chair. "I was brought up on realism. You
know: Faulkner, Hemingway, Cheever."

Kate seemed ready to explode. "Fantasy?" she screamed.
"You think this is a fantasy? This kind of stuff happens every
day."

"Really," Eleanor murmured on, keeping her eyes away
from Kate, "it's just a little too much. That train trip through
Mexico was so bad it was almost comical."

"What about the rich doctor's wife on the East Side who treats her undocumented servants like slaves?" Kate demanded. "Wasn't that realistic enough for you?"

"We don't think of them as servants. They don't wait on us, they just clean the apartment. And we certainly don't treat them like slaves."

There was no point in any further discussion. The story, as we all knew, had been aimed at the man who wasn't there—Brian, whose Val Osbourne was the prototype for Kate's perverted Bill Orly, the abusive cop who would rather exploit a murderess than bring her to justice. What was worse, Kate's impotent sex abuser even looked like Brian, with the high forehead and rimless glasses of a man who might have been a professor instead of a security expert or a cop. She seemed to be peering under Val Osbourne's cheerful exterior, and Brian's, to find a nasty, impotent, and violent personality which bore little resemblance to Val Osbourne and even less to his creator. And the worst part was that Brian wasn't even there to defend himself. The group had sunk to a dangerous all-time low.

Or so I thought.

10

That night I forgot to turn off my cell phone when I went to bed. It rang at 6:00 o'clock the next morning, an hour before my alarm was set to go off. In my groggy state all I knew was that it was Sara and she was babbling incoherently. "It's Brian," she kept saying. "I think Brian's been killed."

"What are you talking about?"

"I was worried about Brian not showing up last night so I looked on the *Daily News* website and there was this guy named Brian fitting his description who got killed a couple of nights ago in a hit and run accident on the Upper West Side. He was a civil engineer with some security consulting firm and—"

"Wait a minute? What was his last name?"

"Maynes. Brian Maynes."

"Jesus," I said in a faltering voice. "That was Brian. Brian Maynes. His office was on the Upper West Side."

Sara and I met for lunch at a quiet Italian place around the corner from her office. I stood up and hugged her when she arrived, and by the time we sat down she was wiping tears from her eyes. "I can't believe this," she said. "First Jackie and now Brian. I can't believe it. What's going on?"

"I don't know," I said, trying to sound steadier than I felt. "It's unbelievable."

"It can't be a coincidence."

"It could be a coincidence. What are the odds of two people in the group dying in the same month? Low, yes, but not astronomically low."

"Almost astronomical, I would say."

"But what's the alternative?"

She grimaced and buried her face in the menu. There was an obvious alternative and we both knew who it was: Eleanor. But we avoided that topic until the waiter had brought our meals.

"Eleanor wrote the script for killing Jackie," I said, fiddling with my pasta. "And we let her get away with it."

"Wait a minute."

"Now we've let her kill Brian too."

"You don't know that," she objected. "You wanted to turn her in for killing Jackie, just based on that story she wrote, and it turned out she had an alibi. She wasn't even in New York that day."

"So she says."

"What makes you think she killed Brian? The *Daily News* said it was an accident. Maybe that's what it was—an accident. Eleanor doesn't even drive."

I leveled my eyes at hers. "You're deluding yourself."

"Why would she kill him?"

"Don't you remember the story he read? His detective Val Osbourne had Eleanor convicted of first degree murder. And the woman she killed was a lot like Jackie."

Sara shook her head and smiled indulgently. "Will, this is the real world we're talking about. People don't kill each other because of some story."

"Maybe some people do." I smiled back, less indulgently. "I think we should call Detective Falcone."

"No," she insisted. "Do you know what can happen to someone if the cops get hold of them? Even a rich lady like Eleanor."

"If there isn't any evidence, they'll let her go."

"If there isn't any evidence, they'll make it up." She reached across the table and touched my hand. "Promise me, Will. Promise me you won't call Falcone."

Sara's Journal
June 29

Now Brian is dead along with Jackie and nobody knows why. Will still wants to blame Eleanor. He says he won't talk to the detective but I don't believe him.

The doctors say Mom could live another six months but I don't believe them either.

Continuation by Will Schaefer

Kate called me that night before I left the office. She was sobbing and she sounded desperate and very drunk. She was at a bar on the far West Side and wanted me to come over and take her home.

It was a surprisingly rough bar for a militant feminist to hang out in, guarded by a bouncer with enough tattoos to scare off a motorcycle gang. He almost bounced me because my sweat-soaked suit and tie didn't comply with the dress code, which required wife beaters, halter tops and leather pants. I'd assumed it was a gay bar, but the first thing I saw when I stepped inside was a row of straight couples in Goth attire making out at the bar (or were they just trying to disentangle their lip and eyebrow piercings?). I could understand why Kate wanted me to take her home, but what was she doing there in the first place?

She threw her arms around me and pulled me into a booth, sobbing. "Will, thanks so much for coming! I couldn't handle this by myself!"

In her stories, Kate always described herself as a warm and wonderful person. That may have been true in her dealings with women, but toward men, myself in particular, she was usually as cold as a bluefish in an ice bucket. When Zelda first introduced us—that was before I started dating Zelda—I was vain enough to perceive her aloofness as a stimulant. I asked her out to dinner and she spent the whole night talking about date rape. But that night, the night after we'd learned of Brian's death, she was a different person. She clutched my hands across the table and drowned me in an outpouring of emotions I didn't know she was capable of. Death will do that to people.

"I see a lot of shocking things in my job," she said after she'd calmed down enough to talk about Brian. "Women beaten, women raped, women murdered by their husbands or boyfriends. But this is really messing me up. I felt physically ill when I heard about Brian. I had to go in the bathroom and throw up."

"I know how you feel."

"It's so horrible. Do you think this is connected with what happened to Jackie?"

"Connected? How could it be connected?"

She squinted skeptically through her tears. "Does the name 'Eleanor' mean anything to you? That story of Brian's—"

"Come on! Eleanor wouldn't do anything like that—"

"What do you know about Eleanor?"

"I'm sure it was just a random accident. A hit and run." I was quoting the arguments I'd dismissed when Sara made them. "Eleanor doesn't even drive."

"How do you know she doesn't drive?"

"Kate, people don't kill each other because of some story."

She tried to smile but only managed to twist her mouth into a defiant grin. "I felt like killing him over that story!"

"I could tell you were upset," I mumbled. "But it wasn't really—"

"I was more than upset! I'm telling you, I wanted to kill him! Literally!" She made a strangling gesture with her clenched fists. "And now he's dead!"

She sank her face into her hands and sobbed again. Was she crying because she'd killed him? I wondered. Or because she'd missed her chance?

I scooted over to her side of the booth and wrapped my arm around her shoulders. "I know you wouldn't kill anybody, Kate. Nobody in the group would kill anybody."

She pulled away. "You think you know us, don't you? You think you know all about everybody in the group?"

"I know you well enough to know you're not murderers. You're like family to me."

Her eyes blazed. "What about Josh? Do you know Josh?"

"As well as anybody could know him."

"Which is like saying you're on intimate terms with somebody from another planet."

"OK, he's a little strange."

"And me—"

You're definitely from another planet, I thought, slipping back into my seat across the table. And it probably isn't Venus.

"What makes you think you know anything about me?"

"Kate"—I smiled my most reassuring smile—"We've known each other for a long time. We went out once, remember?"

"Yeah, I remember," she winced. "You spent the whole time talking about how great you are."

"I'm sorry you remember it that way. The way I—"

"Forget it, Will." She pulled out a handkerchief and daubed at her tears. "Listen, I hear things at the shelter, things you couldn't make up. Every woman who comes in there has been abused in a hundred different ways, and they tell me about it. It's not fiction. In the story I read last night, the part about Eleanor—"

"Eleanor was in your story?"

"What did I call her? Mrs. Gamael?"

"The rich doctor's wife on the East Side?"

"That was Eleanor. One of the women at the shelter used to do cleaning work for her. I'm sure it was Eleanor she was describing. Every detail was the same: the apartment on the East Side, the fat, pompous husband (only he wasn't a doctor, he was a banker like Eleanor's husband), the mean-spirited daughter. And Eleanor herself, treating the immigrants like slaves. I wanted to strangle her last night when she called my story a fantasy. It's a literal transcription of reality, and it's about her. She's an alcoholic, by the way."

"Oh, come on!"

"And she does drive. She's got a Mercedes in the garage but she makes her husband escort her around in a taxi."

"But what makes you so sure it was Eleanor?"

"How many women could there be in New York who fit that description?"

It was hopeless. She was using the same set of facts to identify Eleanor and then, when they didn't fit, to prove she was a liar. I decided to change the subject. "Have you talked to Zelda lately?"

"Zelda stopped talking to me because I didn't drop out of the writers' group when she broke up with you," she sniffed.

"Really?"

"She says you're a much bigger weirdo than anybody realizes."

"In that case I'm glad she stopped talking to you."

"Don't get too comfortable," she smiled, wiping away the last of her tears. "Zelda and I are meeting for a drink next week and she's going to tell me all your secrets."

Brian's funeral was two days later at a big church in Harlem and it was a sad and moving experience. Sara and I arrived together and were welcomed by a solemn but kindly usher who stood beside the church's open doors. In the foyer just inside the doors stood a circle of Brian's friends and relatives with their hands joined together, softly moaning one of those old Southern hymns that wander hopefully between sadness and joy. Some of the people were sobbing, others were calling out prayers or exclamations. No one knew us and we must have looked out of place to them but they understood that we were Brian's friends and they opened their hands to us and welcomed us into their circle as if we were part of the family. When I explained to Brian's aunt, who stood beside me, that we were from Brian's writers' group, I was answered with a kindly but uncomprehending stare. Probably no one there even knew about his writing.

Inside the church the mourners filed past the open casket for a last glimpse of Brian, some kneeling in prayer beside the coffin, many in tears. A procession of sobbing women huddled around his mother and his two children, a boy in a blue suit and a little girl in pigtails who were just old enough to do what was expected of them but not quite old enough to understand what was going on. I slipped discreetly into one of the middle pews but Sara followed the line forward. When she reached the coffin she dropped to her knees and crossed herself elaborately while she prayed. I had never seen her look more beautiful.

By the time the service began the church was filled to overflowing. There were hymns and prayers and tributes led by the pastor, who spoke eloquently about aspects of Brian's life he had never revealed to our group: his work with abused children and prisoners and his devotion to his faith and family. It was moving but I felt like a hypocrite, as I always do in church. And with Sara beside me I began to feel like a spiritual voyeur. It thrilled me to hear her singing the hymns and joining in the prayers and responses even though they meant nothing to me. Her singing voice was high and childlike and altogether different from the way she spoke; it projected a religious devotion, so out of keeping with her usual aloofness, that made her seem more mysterious and alluring than ever. Like Brian, I realized; I knew very little about her.

When the service ended and everyone stood up to leave, I noticed Kate and Eleanor in one of the pews behind us, talking quietly with Josh, who had finally put his black suit to good use. When Eleanor stood up she glanced toward me with an innocent, kindly smile that sent a shiver down my spine. And then I had a minor shock. In the last row, shoulders against the wall, stood Detective Falcone, gazing over the crowd in our direction. He had his eyes on Eleanor, I told myself. Or was it Kate or Josh? But no, I finally understood as we all began to file out—he was looking right at me.

Outside the church, Sara and Eleanor and Kate hugged each other while Josh and I looked sober and stoical. Looking sober was no problem at that hour of the day, but as far as I was concerned wearing a suit in equatorial weather went beyond the acceptable limits of stoicism. I loosened my tie, wishing I could tear off my jacket or even my shirt. The sooner we found an air conditioned cab the happier I would be.

Kate was frantically telling the other women about something that happened the night before. Apparently someone—Kate assumed it was a rapist—had followed her home from work, a figure shapeless and almost indiscernible in the twilight shadows, and later, when she walked a few blocks to meet some friends at a bar, she had the sensation that she was being followed. Sickened with fear, she turned around and saw the stalker again, about a block behind her, wearing a floppy hat and raincoat on a night that was clear and unbearably hot.

"Was it a man or a woman?" I asked, glancing involuntarily at Eleanor.

"Of course it was a man," Kate snapped. "Do you know any female rapists?"

"How do you know he was stalking you?"

"You know when you're being stalked. Whenever I turned around, there he was, still a block behind me, barely visible behind a tree or under an awning, and when I went another block I'd turn around and there he was again."

"What did you do?" asked Sara.

"I ducked into the nearest bar. It was a dive, full of creepy drunks with their eyes glued to a baseball game, but I didn't care. I just stood inside the doorway and called a cab. The driver wasn't too happy when he found out we were only going three blocks but I never felt more relieved in my life."

Eleanor reached out and gave Kate's hand a squeeze. "Kate," she said, "if you need to go out tonight, just give me a call. I'll send Howard over to pick you up."

"I'm not going anywhere tonight," Kate said, pulling her hand away. "But thanks anyway, Eleanor."

"By the way," I said, "I was wondering if anybody has been getting those anonymous phone calls in the middle of the night."

"Mine stopped," said Kate, suddenly subdued. Her eyes turned away, toward the door of the church, where a few mourners were still filing out.

"When did they stop?"

"About the time Brian died," she said softly.

"Well, mine haven't stopped," I said.

"And we've started getting them," Eleanor said. She glanced at me anxiously as if I had demanded an explanation. "Howard's a light sleeper and he's often up at that hour."

"How many rings?" I asked.

"Three," she said. "Howard says it always rings three times and then stops."

11

We left the funeral in separate cabs, Kate and Eleanor and Josh in one, Sara and I in the other. Sara and I had arrived together and sat together, and I wondered if the others had started to notice that our relationship was a little special. As a matter of fact I wondered if Sara had started to notice. She was so elusive and detached that I never really knew what she was thinking or whether she knew or cared how I felt about her.

It was still before noon when I had the cab driver drop us off by the Frick Gallery so we could walk through Central Park on the way back to our offices. The winding pathways in the park were full of young mothers with strollers, groups of skipping little girls and slow-motion matrons walking tiny dogs.

Sara had been quiet on the cab ride and as soon as we wandered down a secluded path I found out why. "Will," she said, "the detective who came to your apartment to tell us about Jackie—"

"Detective Falcone?"

"Yes. He was standing in the back of the church."

"I saw him," I said.

"Why didn't you say anything?"

"I don't know. I'm afraid he suspects someone in the group."

"You mean Eleanor?"

"He was staring at me."

Sara stopped and turned to face me, and I had the uncomfortable impression that in spite of her commitment to civil liberties she was reading my mind. "You're thinking about turning Eleanor in, aren't you?" she asked me.

"I've been wrestling with that possibility."

"Why? There isn't any evidence that she killed Brian or had anything to do with his death."

"Except there is a reason to believe she killed Jackie."

"What reason? Her story? That isn't evidence."

"It's the only evidence we've got."

"What about the fact that she was in Vermont the day Jackie got killed?"

"I wish I knew if that was true."

Sara took a moment to rein in her anger. It was our first argument and I had never seen her look so fierce or so beautiful. "Listen to me, Will," she finally said. "I'm writing a story right now that you or someone else might find frightening or even incriminating. If I can't bring it to the group without being turned in to the police, you're going to be looking for at least one new member."

"I understand," I said. "That's why I've been wrestling."

We resumed our walk in the park until we found an isolated bench near a pond, where we sat for a while watching the ducks. They swam towards us and even waddled onto the bank, as if handouts from humans were an entitlement program. Finally some tourists obliged by tossing an entire sandwich into the pond, triggering a shameless display of ornithological greed. It reflected poorly, I thought, not only on the ducks but on some seagulls who had apparently been using the ducks as decoys. Meanwhile Sara and I talked about Brian's funeral, which we'd both found uplifting. In particular (though I kept this thought to myself) I had been inspired by the sight of Sara kneeling in prayer beside the coffin. "I didn't realize you were so religious," I said.

"I'm not, except at funerals. The rest of the time I'm like everyone else."

"Meaning what?"

"An egoist. Isn't that the universal religion?"

I laughed. "Does egoism include belief in an afterlife?"

"Unfortunately not," she smiled. "That's what the other religions are for."

She stood up and continued down the path, expecting me to follow her, which I did. "I noticed you weren't joining in the prayers or hymns," she said. "Are you a full time egoist?"

I laughed again. "Absolutely. I got a lifetime supply of religion when I was a kid in southern Illinois."

"I thought you were from Missouri."

"Well, right across the river. They had the same religion on both sides of the river."

"Was that the reason you left home?"

"It was one of the reasons, I guess. There were lots of worse things going on."

We stopped walking for a minute to let a little boy wobble by on his bike. "How old were you?" she asked. "Seventeen? Eighteen? What did you do?"

"I did all the things writers are supposed to do, according to the little biographies they put on dust jackets. Though at the time I didn't know that was why I was doing them."

"Such as?"

"Bartender in San Francisco, lumberjack in Oregon, short order cook in Alaska. I even worked a season on a fishing boat in the Aleutians. Then I headed south and spent two years wandering through Central and South America, where it was sex, drugs and barely escaping with my life. Somehow I ended up in Houston and that's where the story starts to take on some direction."

"What direction?"

"The direction of being here today with you, I guess."

We bought sandwiches and Cokes from a vendor and sat on a stone ledge and had a little picnic. It was almost 1:00 o'clock by now and I was trying to remember what I was supposed to do at the office that afternoon.

"You still seem troubled," Sara said. "I'm sorry if I got a little worked up about Eleanor."

"No, it's not that. It's just that with all this going on, I've been having a hard time concentrating on my work."

"You mean at the office? Or your writing?"

"Both. Maybe I need a muse."

"A muse?"

"Some beautiful woman who whispers in my ear while I'm working."

She frowned. "Why does a muse have to be beautiful?"

"I don't know, it's just—"

"Why does it have to be a woman?"

"No reason," I admitted, jumping up from the ledge. "That's why I've got Martin. He's my proctor in the examination room of life."

I crumpled my garbage and conspicuously checked the time on my watch. "In fact, I'd better get back to the office right now. My boss has been sending me frantic text messages about every five minutes."

We headed down a curving path toward 59th Street, where a demonstration was in progress. A group of bearded young men wearing colorful headgear were chanting and carrying signs that said 'Death to America' while tourists snapped pictures on their cell phones. The locals stepped around the demonstrators as if they were no more noteworthy than a pile of horse manure.

"It's a great country," I observed.

My observation seemed to touch a nerve in Sara. She turned toward me with an intense stare that made me wonder if she was going to join the demonstration. "The biggest problem facing immigrants today isn't finding a job or getting enough to eat," she said. "It's a kind of existential alienation. These are single-minded, self-disciplined people who have focused every ounce of their attention for years and years on the goal of getting to America—only to discover, once they're here, that their purposefulness no longer serves any purpose. In America it's considered passé to believe in anything."

"What happened to the American Dream?"

"Everybody woke up. And now they wish they could go back to sleep."

We walked another half block, stopping to inspect the renovated Plaza Hotel. "I was six years old when we came to this country," she said. "But I could remember enough of the craziness we had to go through to get here that by the age of ten I realized that the rest of my life would seem boring and unreal by comparison. Which doesn't take a huge leap of the imagination when you're going to a fancy private school in the suburbs and your biggest intellectual challenge is how to look cool in your field hockey kilt."

"I'm sure you looked terrific in your field hockey kilt." Was that an inappropriate remark? Fortunately she ignored it.

"My father worked hard to establish himself so he could afford to send us to the right schools and summer camps," she went on. "And his hard work paid off when I got into Yale. My mother never really mastered English and she managed to make 'Yale' sound like a place they put criminals. But there was nobody within a hundred miles who didn't know I was going to Yale."

"I must have still been in Houston then."

She nodded, disregarding any irony she might have detected in my voice. "I majored in Art History and did a semester in Rome my junior year. That was enough to get my foot in the door at Abrams and since then I've been with three other publishing houses. It's basically media work but I'm hoping if I stay around long enough I can find my way over to editorial."

We were a block from Sara's office building and not a moment too soon, I thought. Childhood memories, career paths, job satisfaction—we were getting into second-date territory and this was a perfect time to make the segue. "Would you like to have dinner Saturday night?" I asked her.

She gave me her most inscrutable smile. "Need a little inspiration?"

The muse theme again. I didn't bite. "No, just a nice dinner."

"I'll think about it."

We exchanged casual goodbyes in front of her building— almost too casual, it seemed to me, as if we were trying to extricate ourselves from an unexpectedly intimate afternoon. We'd survived our first argument without resolving the issue that had caused it: what to do about Eleanor. That issue, along with my conscience, I would have to wrestle with in private.

As I walked down Madison Avenue toward my office I tried to focus on what I needed to do that afternoon. My boss, Bob Tedder, had been sending me messages from his iPhone all morning. Martin had been frantically trying to reach me on my cell phone. But as I walked, all I could think about was the ambiguous smile I'd seen on Eleanor's face as she stood up to leave. A question ran through my mind, over and over again, like the melody of one of those old Southern hymns: What would the people at Brian's funeral have thought if they knew his killer was sitting right there in one of the pews?

12

Reporting to Bob Tedder was like raising a handicapped child. You had to keep him from getting confused or upset and shelter him from failure, protecting his self-esteem at all costs. You had to steer him clear of situations where he might be judged harshly or unfairly. You had to do his homework for him and make sure he got full credit for everything you did. If he threw a tantrum, you had to humor him until it passed and make sure you never mentioned it again. And if anyone asked, you had to tell them how lucky you were to have him as your boss.

Bob was in his mid-forties, a little paunchy, bespectacled, with a hairline that was receding at about the same rate as the Arctic ice. He avoided confrontation and spoke in a barely audible monotone as if he didn't want to attract attention to himself. But behind his bland exterior he was the most ruthlessly calculating man I've ever known. For everything he said or did, and I mean *everything*—even the most casual, seemingly meaningless gesture or comment—there was a reason. If he arrived at the office a little early or a little late, there was a reason; if he spoke up at a meeting or held his silence, or smiled or made a joke, there was a reason; if he praised your work or ignored it, recommended you for a promotion or suggested that you take some time off, there was a reason. Sometimes you didn't realize what the reason was until long afterwards; weeks or months could go by before it dawned on you why he'd done what he did or said what he said. But there was always a reason, and it was always the same reason—to protect and promote the career of Bob Tedder. Every detail of his life was crafted with lapidary skill to advance that goal, even as he cultivated an image that was precisely the opposite. I seemed to be the only one who saw him for what he really was, but of course that was part of the deception. His devotion to his own self-interest was so complete that it was invisible, like a dictator's Big Lie, obvious to all but impossible to call attention to without exposing yourself to danger.

Especially when dealing with higher-ups, Bob's preferred mode of communication was sentence fragments arranged in 16-point type on PowerPoint slides—"Bullet points," he called them, possibly revealing more about their true nature than he intended. "Putting subjects and verbs together in the same sentence," he said one day, shaking his head. "Highly problematic. Safer to stick to bullet points." We were riding up on the elevator to break the news to our CEO, Milton Babst, that an anti-globalization group had threatened to disrupt the annual stockholders' meeting. "Your chance to shine," Bob said as we stepped off the elevator.

Mr. Babst greeted us like a couple of plumbers who'd come to fix his toilet. "Well!" he blurted without rising or asking us to sit down. "What's the problem?"

"Threatened disruption," Bob muttered.

He nodded in my direction, and I realized that I was expected to supply the rest of his message. "By anti-globalization protestors," I added quickly. "At the stockholders' meeting."

"What the hell are they protesting about?" Babst demanded.

"Jobs," said Bob, rolling his eyes toward me.

"They say we're hurting the economy," I explained, "by exporting all the high-paying jobs to Asia—"

"That's ridiculous!" Babst sprang from his chair, glaring at me as if I were one of the protesters. "In the past five years Zunax has created more high-paying jobs in the United States than anywhere else in the world. My job, for instance. And yours, Bob. Hell, we have over a hundred vice presidents!"

"Can't disagree," Bob agreed.

"And what about all those bean counters on the fifteenth floor? The Finance Department. Do you realize how much we pay those morons?"

"Manufacturing jobs," Bob suggested, returning to his mental slide deck.

"I think they're more concerned about skilled manufacturing jobs going to China and India," I said, taking the cue.

"Damn it! How can you say that?" Babst poked his forefinger into my chest with a look that defied me to contradict him. "We have factories all over North America."

"Brooklyn," said Bob.

"That's right. There's a factory right in Brooklyn, as a matter of fact. Maybe you should take the protestors over there and let them see what it's like to work for a living."

"Great feedback," Bob concurred, edging toward the door.

"Of course it's great feedback."

I turned around and realized that Bob Tedder had slipped out behind me.

Babst shot me one last scowl and sat back down at his desk. "Can I help you with something?"

When I returned to the office after Brian's funeral, I
encountered Martin in the building lobby, headed out to
Lexington Avenue. He was wearing a jacket and tie and
carrying a briefcase, all recent affectations which I hoped
signaled that he was looking for a new job. He had to leave
early for a doctor's appointment, he said, but not to worry—
he was taking work home. I don't know why he thought I
would believe that. He didn't do any work. How could he be
taking it home?

"Tedder's in a twit," he warned me in his most
confidential tone. "Some kind of crisis."

"One of his dalliances?"

"No. I think it's financial."

Before I could deal with Bob Tedder's crisis there was a
phone call I needed to make. Eleanor's husband Howard was
an old friend of Milton Babst's and did some consulting work
for Zunax. I wondered if I could use that connection to see
if Eleanor's Vermont alibi held any water. I dialed Howard's
office from a conference room and his secretary answered,
sounding pert and eager to please. "This is Bob Martin
calling from Zunax," I said, giving the first name that popped
into my head. "We're trying to arrange a meeting with Mr.
Babst and some other people, and I just wanted to check on
Howard's availability."

"Sure," she replied. "What day were you thinking of?"

"How does his schedule look for two o'clock next
Thursday afternoon?"

"The seventh? He'd have to call in from his house in
Vermont."

"How about the day before? Could he come to the
meeting on Wednesday?"

"It would have to be early in the day. He drives up to Vermont on Wednesday."

I allowed myself a folksy chuckle. "Can't blame him for wanting to get away from the city. But couldn't he be a little flexible? Mr. Babst would really like to have him there."

"He can call in. That's not usually a problem."

"He must be pretty adamant about his trips to Vermont. Does he go up there every week?"

"Like clockwork," she said, sounding a little less pert and eager to please. "Wednesday through Sunday. Every week after Memorial Day."

"But you know," I pursued, "glancing back over my calendar, it looks like Howard was here for a meeting on Thursday, June the ninth. Is that possible?"

"What was your name again?"

Bob Tedder summoned me to his office the minute I sat down at my desk. What we had wasn't exactly a crisis, he explained, but without careful handling it could turn into one. Second quarter earnings—to be announced in mid-July— would not meet Zunax's published projections. We had no hard data as yet. The challenge was to manage Wall Street's expectations without revealing any unpleasant facts.

I stepped back to my office and closed the door so I could concentrate, and after two hours of work I had crafted a press release I was ready to share with Bob and his staff. It was the usual chowder of corporatespeak, legalese and meaningless statistics, no more bland or impenetrable than what a hundred other companies ladle out to investors on a daily basis. I printed out several copies and took them into the windowless conference room where we reviewed our drafts with the team. In a few minutes I was joined by Bob, who as usual seemed distracted by more important matters on his iPhone, and Julie Kim, his former secretary and current love interest, who, in an unrelated development, had recently been promoted to Senior Director of Corporate Communications. Julie had straight black hair and stiletto eyes and she winced as she read my press release as if it was giving her a migraine attack. I felt anxious and vulnerable, like a new member reading his first story to the writers' group.

"I didn't like the part about the factory in Michigan being sold to the Chinese," Julie Kim said. "That's really going to offend people."

"But it's true, isn't it?" I said.

"True?" Bob chuckled, glancing at his iPhone. "Look here. Ten million dollars in revenue last quarter. Couldn't very well be closed, could it?"

"Whether it's closed or not," Julie said, "we can't put that in the press release."

"Agreed," said Bob. "Now another point. Employees. You say 25,000 worldwide. Same as last year?"

"Last year we said we had 50,000," Julie recalled, frowning in my direction.

I stood my ground. "The 25,000 figure came from Human Resources."

"Can't be right, can it?" Bob asked.

"No way," Julie said. "Let's change it back to 50,000."

Bob smiled his avuncular smile, tolerant but a little disappointed. "One more thing, Will. The tone of this document—a little harsh, don't you think? Just a dry recital of facts, makes the company sound cold and uncaring. You notice that, Julie?"

"Absolutely."

"Not a criticism, Will. Just a little constructive feedback. For instance, 'The Company projects earnings growth of greater than 10% from operations in Southeast Asia'—can't we sort of …put a human face on that?"

"Well, those are the sneaker factories in Vietnam. You know, where the kids—"

Julie cut me off. "How about this: 'We are confident that our efforts to combat the exploitation of children in Southeast Asia will result in double-digit growth in that region.'"

"Better," Bob nodded. "But—is that the best we can do?"

"No, you're right," Julie said. "How about this: 'In an effort to improve the health and safety of children who have been shamefully exploited by our competitors in Southeast Asia, the Company has launched an innovative program to provide free medical and dental care to its employees in that region.'"

"Much better," Bob agreed. "Don't you think so, Will?"

"But… have we actually done any of these things?"

They both looked away as if I had made an impolite noise.

Bob glanced at his watch. "Gotta jump. Two of you can handle this. Excellent work." This was one of his favorite tricks, leaving a meeting early so he could disavow it or take credit for it, as the need arose. He stopped in the doorway and flashed a boyish grin. "Still have to say something about the expected drop in earnings, don't you think, Will?"

"I'll check with Finance," I said.

He waved that idea aside. "Bean counters! You'll never get anything useful out of them."

"Then what do you want me to do?"

"Just handle it. I'm sure you'll think of something."

13

Sara's Journal
July 1

Will and I have a lot in common. He even lies about what state he's from. He calls my writing minimalist, but his is minimalist to the point of non-existence. I can't find his stories published anywhere. I publish under a different name, he says, without telling what that name is. I could say that too. I could be anyone I want to be.

He thinks he needs a muse. Maybe I'll be the lucky girl. If only I were beautiful enough, maybe I could inspire him to write one of his corporate press releases! LOL. We keep having the same argument about Eleanor. Our first conflict—is that where the story begins? He'd make a good character in one of his stories, if he ever wrote any: likeable but deeply flawed. He criticized Jackie for not loving her characters enough, but what about him? Does he even have any empathy for real people like Eleanor? Or does he see people (including himself) as if they were characters in some complicated story, to be manipulated by him as the puppet master? I shouldn't say that (but that's what this journal is, isn't it—the place where I can say all the things I shouldn't say?). He's a nice enough guy in his own way. It's just that sometimes I feel he's trying too hard, like he's saving cats and running down child abusers just to earn his way into Heaven as a likeable character.

July 2

Called Will and told him I couldn't have dinner with him. Had to spend extra time with Mom even though she's driving me nuts. She made me spend all afternoon watching soap operas. She loves them because they go on forever, and when a character dies it only means she found a better job.

More ideas for the story: It's closing time at Celeste's Unisex. Nika is the last to leave, locking the door behind her. Stepping across the street comes a tall, full-bearded man in a black suit. He looks like a rabbi, his eyes deep and dark with the fear of God.

Excuse me, he says. My name is Steve Tennenbaum. I'm Mario's manager.

Mario's manager? Mario who?

I'm sorry. Mario Migliori, the artist. He's the customer who was banned from your shop.

That wasn't my idea.

Rules are rules, he shrugs, breaking into a manager's smile, manipulative and shameless yet somehow irresistible. Actually I wanted to talk to you about something else.

I've got to go.

Uninvited, he dogs her steps as far as the subway station at Canal Street. He says:

Mario would like to take you out to dinner. Or to a show, if you prefer. Whatever you want to do. He wants to get to know you better.

Why?

He's a romantic, a bit of a fantasist. He gets his artistic energy from beautiful women.

You sound more like a pimp than a manager.

The manager laughs, then he says:

To be quite honest, there's nothing sexual about this. It's artistic. He can't work.

Nika smiles to herself as she remembers the pathetic scene at the Pergamon Gallery. Mario crawling around on all fours and leering after her like a dog, pressing his nose against the glass. Nothing sexual.

Mario's an important figure in the art world, Steve Tennenbaum argues. He's recognized as the father of aleatoric minimalism.

Whatever that means.

He captures little pieces of reality and freezes them in time and space. The goal is to find the smallest number of random events, with the least amount of human intervention, that can be accepted as a work of art.

What does he want with me?

He needs a muse. An artist can't work without a muse.

At the subway, edging into the crowd, Nika bobs down the stairs and feels herself being sucked through the turnstile and onto the platform like debris swirling down a sink. Steve Tennenbaum clings to her like a shadow, his black suit drenched with sweat. She turns to confront him.

Mario wants to take me to dinner so he can hang pieces of electrical tape from the ceiling? Is this a joke?

I'm sorry if you feel insulted. No offense was intended.

I'd be less insulted if you told me he wanted to have sex with me.

The manager smiles uncomfortably and opens his mouth to reply but the train comes roaring and screeching in beside them. As soon as the doors open she dives into the car and watches the surge of exiting passengers sweep him away.

14

Continuation by Will Schaefer

My dinner date with Sara for Saturday night never took place. At the last minute she remembered a prior commitment to take her mother to the opera, and when I suggested a different night she was non-committal. I spent a depressed weekend wondering if she was one of those *femmes fatales* (I had known quite a few of them) whose very aloofness is their allure. One positive development: the heat wave had finally broken. On Saturday afternoon a tremendous thunderstorm raged over the city like an aerial bombardment. The power went out, and for three hours the fate of the world seemed to hang in the balance. When I stepped outside I expected to see the neighborhood reduced to rubble. Instead it was only steamy and wet, with a refreshing breeze blowing in from the west. The collective meltdown we seemed to be headed for had been averted, at least for a couple of days. Monday was the Fourth of July and there was a chance that we would get to enjoy our holiday before the end came.

Meanwhile I was becoming obsessed with the phone calls. Before Jackie died, the phone always rang once and then stopped. Then after Jackie's death and before Brian's, it rang twice. And before I even heard about Brian—before anyone but the killer could have known he was dead—it had started ringing three times. The calls weren't tallying the deaths, I realized; they were predicting them. On Saturday night, having been ditched by Sara, I kept my phone turned on and sat up drinking Jack Daniel's, waiting for it to ring. One o'clock came and went, then two, then three. I made a pot of coffee and was able to keep myself awake until 5:00, when it was almost starting to get light. I collapsed on the bed and within ten minutes the phone rang. I was up like a shot, clinging to my pillow and trembling more in anger than in fright as I listened. Once, twice, three times. More than ever I was sure the caller was Zelda. I realized how stupid I'd been: all night long she'd been watching and waiting for me to go to sleep. All she had to do was slip down the back stairs and glance up at my window to see if I was waiting up for the call, and when I turned out the lights she waited just long enough to lull me into a dreamless sleep. I wanted to run downstairs and pound on her door and skin her alive but of course Wolfgang would be there, scratching and growling and trying to chew his way toward me to settle old scores.

Going back to sleep was out of the question: At 8:00 o'clock I had my appointment with Dr. G. I slipped on my sandals and padded over to McDonald's for some Egg McMuffins and vast quantities of coffee. Then I buzzed home, showered, even shaved—after all, he was a doctor— and headed downtown for a game of chess. Why was I doing this? I knew why, and it sounded pathetic, even to me. It had nothing to do with chess. I needed somebody to talk to.

Dr. G sat straddling his suitcase with the chess pieces set up on the end of the upturned carton, the empty shoe box for collecting captured pieces, and the laundry timer ready to crank into action. He grinned a little more broadly than usual as he explained that—for patriotic reasons—special Fourth of July Weekend rates would apply: $25 for a checkmate within thirty minutes, $15 for each additional quarter hour or portion thereof. For the holiday he had planted a small American flag at each end of the park bench and exchanged his red stocking cap for a New York Yankees hat which he wore backwards over his stiff shock of white hair.

He set the timer for thirty minutes and I told him everything that had happened that week, just as I've written it down here: Kate's story, Brian's death and funeral, my conversations with Sara (omitting the part about our dinner date), my strong suspicion of Eleanor's guilt and my investigation of her alibi. As I spoke he frowned down at the chess board in deep concentration and hardly appeared to be listening, except for an occasional "Uh, huh!" or "Is that so?" (and even an "Amen!" when I described how beautiful Sara looked kneeling in prayer at Brian's funeral). When I had finished, he moved his king's bishop into attack position, eyeing two of my pawns. "How do all that make you feel?" he asked.

"What do you mean?"

"Ain't that what a doctor's suppose to ask? How do that make you feel?"

"Well, I don't—"

"I mean, if you rather keep it all bottled up inside, you can do that, but it ain't healthy. You got to get in touch with your inner child!"

I stared back incredulously as he nabbed one of my pawns and opened a line of attack on my king's rook. "I stay in touch with mine," he grinned.

"OK," I said, "it all makes me pretty upset. These people are my friends. Two of them have been murdered in the past two weeks, and another one probably killed them. So, yes, I'm pretty upset about it." I moved my rook forward two spaces to stave off the attack by his bishop.

"You're making progress," he nodded, capturing the rook with his queen's knight. "But maybe what you need to make is some new friends. Even the folks I hang out with ain't as bad as this writers' group—we get maybe one murder a month, at the most—and we're living on the street."

I made a few pointless moves and in a heartbeat three more of my pawns had disappeared into the shoe box. I wanted to defend my friends in the group but I knew he would destroy them as mercilessly as he eliminated my pawns.

"So when you gonna ask Sara out?" he asked.

"Well," I hesitated, "I already did. We were supposed to go out last night."

"Suppose to? What happened?"

"It turned out she'd promised to take her mother to the opera."

If I had any illusions about Sara's excuse, Dr. G blew them away, along with my queen's bishop, with one flip of his wrist. "Now I don't go to too many operas," he said, dropping the bishop into the shoe box. "Sure, once in a while I get the urge to take the old tuxedo out of storage and strut out for the evening to hear folks yodeling in a language I can't understand—but like I say, I don't do it too often. But I do know one thing: it ain't something you do on the spur of the moment. You got to get your tickets about a year ahead and if you bring your mama she's gonna need a hair-do that takes about three days to set. So if somebody tells you they just remembered—"

"OK, I take your point. Maybe Sara was lying."

He snatched up one of my horses and dropped it into the shoe box. "Now we're getting somewhere."

"I'd rather not talk about my relationship with Sara," I said.

"Why not?" His yellow cat's eyes glimmered in the morning sunlight. "Ain't it important?"

"Of course it's important. It just—"

"It's why you here at eight o'clock in the morning looking like death warmed over instead of springing out of that gal's bed like a happy jackrabbit and not wasting your time with an old fool like me."

"It just doesn't have anything to do with why people are dying."

"I certainly hope not," he said, his grin widening, "cause if someday you don't show up for your appointment, I'd have to charge you anyway." He pointed to a rusted metal sign propped up on the park bench that read, *24 hour notice of cancellation required.*

We both laughed but my merriment was cut short when I surveyed the wreckage on my side of the chess board. In fifteen minutes I'd lost four pawns, a horse, a bishop and a rook, and enemy forces had penetrated deep inside my territory. My only hope was to go on the offensive. I moved my queen forward, aiming at one of his horses.

"Was Mr. Laurel and Hardy at the funeral?" Dr. G asked, moving his horse away without hesitation as if he'd been expecting my move.

"Howard? No, just Eleanor, along with the others in the group."

"Check!" Now the horse menaced my king, leaving me no choice but to move the king one space sideways.

"Now here's the question I'd be asking myself if I was you." He bored his eyes into mine as his fingers hovered over the board. "If that fat boy go up to Vermont every Wednesday—which is what they told you, right?—do he take his wife along with him or not? Because this young man

Brian's funeral, you say, was on Friday, and Eleanor's there, she ain't in Vermont or anywhere near it."

"That's right."

He rushed his queen forward, aiming it directly at my king. "Check!"

I searched desperately for some means of escape. The only thing I could do was block his queen with my remaining horse.

"So what I want to be asking," he went on, nudging the queen one space to the side, "is where is this woman now? She in New York? Because if she's in New York, then how you know she's not in New York that other weekend even though her husband be up there milking cows or chopping wood or whatever else they do in Vermont?"

Having no other move, I captured one of his pawns with my queen and dropped it into the shoe box. "That's a good point."

He laughed. "Course it's a good point. I didn't get to be a doctor for nothing." And with a slight movement of his bishop, he cornered my king between his queen and one of my own pawns just as the timer went off. "Checkmate!"

I stared at the board in disbelief as he reached into the shoebox and started setting up the pieces for the next game.

"That be $25—holiday rates—if you don't mind, sir."

As I fumbled in my pocket for the money I became aware of someone standing behind me, a lanky teenager wearing white shorts and a pair of basketball sneakers the size of snowshoes.

"Now one other thing, before we quit," Dr. G said, "and I won't charge you for this, cause you should've thought of it yourself. The young man who had the funeral—Brian was his name? Didn't you tell me last week about another African-American that got killed on the same street?"

"Yes. Brian told me about that the last time I spoke to him. I knew the guy."

"Another accident?"

"That's what they said but I don't believe it."

"If it wasn't an accident it shoots a big hole in your case against Eleanor, don't it? Which has Eleanor wanting to kill Brian cause of how he made her look in that story he wrote."

"I'm not following you."

"Look here. When that other brother got run down like a dog outside Brian's building—no doubt cause the driver thought one black man look exactly like any other—at that time Brian still didn't read his story to the group, did he? So whoever killed Brian was already trying to do it before Brian read that story."

"But what I'm wondering—"

He stood up and with his most unctuous smile reached over to greet the lanky teenager, who was evidently his next client.

"Our time's up for today."

I fled back uptown, stung by another humiliating defeat but nevertheless convinced that my $25 had been well spent. Talking to Dr. G had cleared some of the cobwebs from my mind, and he'd connected a few dots that I had left dangling in space. I could no longer pretend that Sara stood me up to take her mother to the opera. This realization, which should have been obvious, cast a cloud over my trust in Sara, including her dogged defense of Eleanor. And the status of Eleanor as a suspect seemed more problematic than ever.

Her alibi, as Dr. G had pointed out, was more her husband's than her own, yet she could not have been motivated to kill Brian by the story he read if the earlier hit-and-run attempt—which occurred before he read it—had been aimed at Brian. After another half-gallon of coffee at Starbucks, and probably under its influence, I decided to pay a surprise visit to the East Side.

Eleanor's building was guarded by a sweaty doorman who looked like the drum major in a marching band. After I signed my name in a spiral notebook, he called upstairs and pointed toward the elevator, which I rode to the 24th floor. Eleanor met me outside her apartment. "Is something the matter?"

"Yeah, something's the matter," I said. "We've had two people killed."

Her eyes widened. "Two more people?"

"No, the same two. I just wanted to talk to you. Mind if I come in?"

"Oh," she hesitated. "Howard isn't here."

"That's OK. I didn't come to see Howard."

She led me through a carpeted foyer into a spacious living room furnished with sofas and chairs that might have belonged to Marie Antoinette, with a spectacular view of the East River gleaming in from the other end. That didn't surprise me: You have to be very rich to afford such beautiful views and such hideous furniture. But I was startled to find another person in the room—a young woman of about twenty-five who sat motionless in a wheelchair with an odd expression on her face.

"This is my daughter Dorothy," Eleanor smiled. "Dorothy, this is my friend Will Schaefer."

Dorothy smiled and said something I couldn't understand.

"Dorothy and I have been enjoying this beautiful morning without the necessity of going outside, haven't we, Dorothy?"

Dorothy nodded and grunted again.

"Can I get you a drink?" Eleanor asked me. "I was just about to pour myself a little glass of wine."

And not her first glass of the day, I realized, even though it was 11:00 o'clock on a Sunday morning. Her wine glass—a tall one that stood on the coffee table beside a large decanter and the *Sunday Times* book review section—was either half-full or half-empty. Since I'm a pessimist I'll say it was half-empty; in fact it was more than half-empty. Eleanor was a drinker.

"Are you surprised to find Dorothy here?" she asked as we sat down.

"A little surprised. You've never mentioned a daughter. Except—"

"Except what?"

"In your stories there's usually a daughter, but she's not very nice. Sort of a monster, in fact."

"And not handicapped, as Dorothy has been all her life."

"I didn't know."

"Why should you have known? You're always telling us not to infer anything about a writer's private life from their stories."

It was an awkward moment but Eleanor was a gracious lady and she let me off with a skeptical smile. "Now that you mention it," I said, "I could do with a small glass of wine."

"Certainly."

She poured me a large one and refilled hers almost to the brim. We raised our glasses in a silent toast of friendship.

"So Howard's not here this weekend?" I asked.

"No, he's up in Vermont. He goes up there like clockwork, Wednesday to Sunday every week in the summer. Dorothy and I usually go too, but this week, you know, because of the funeral—"

"Sure. That was nice of you to stay home so you could attend the funeral."

"Brian was one of my favorites. We had similar tastes. We both loved the great writers: Tolstoy, Faulkner, Hemingway—they've never been surpassed, have they? And he trusted my judgment. He would often email his stories so I could read them and give him my comments before our meetings."

I choked a little on my wine. "Really?"

"Is there something wrong with that?"

"No, not at all." I set my glass down and coughed, as if my problem had to do with the mechanics of swallowing. "I just didn't know anyone in the group did that. Did Brian send you his last story ahead of time?"

"You know, I can't remember," she smiled. "No, I don't think he did."

"You don't remember?"

She looked away, as if embarrassed by the memory. "That story was sort of offensive. I don't think he wanted to show it to me."

She refilled my wine glass and used that as an excuse to top off her own. Fueled by the wine, we had a spirited discussion of the weather, the crowds at the beaches, the lack of classical music on the radio, the plight of the newspapers, and the brutal holiday traffic that Howard would face if he decided to stay in Vermont another day and return home on the Fourth. The wine showed in her color (high), her speech (loud), and her attitude (alternately giddy and sarcastic, especially when the subject was her husband).

"Do you have a house in Vermont?" I asked.

"A house? More like a run-down chicken coop." She laughed. "Howard bought it a couple of years ago, against my better judgment."

"It sounds idyllic."

"If you think squalor and isolation are idyllic. The place is on a dirt road about ten miles from the nearest town. You can be up there for the whole weekend and not see a living soul."

I watched her face, wondering if she realized she'd just weakened her alibi. If she felt any anxiety she was an expert at concealing it. "I'm surprised that Howard leaves you here all by yourself."

Her lips tightened with annoyance. "I have Dorothy."

It was my turn to be embarrassed. "I'm sorry. Do the two of you get out much?"

"We go out all the time, don't we, Dorothy?"

Dorothy had fallen asleep in the wheelchair, her head cocked awkwardly to one side. Eleanor rushed over to adjust her position and she woke up, moaning unintelligibly.

"Where I go, Dorothy goes," Eleanor said, smiling unpleasantly at Dorothy as if warning her to keep quiet. "Except when her nurse in on duty. Isn't that right, dear?"

"Oh." I stood up to leave. "Do you drive?"

"Of course I drive. I even own a car." She took my elbow and escorted me to the door. "Would you like to examine it for paint chips to see if they match the ones found on Brian's body?"

Sara's Journal
July 3

More ideas for the story. It's coming together.

At Celeste's Unisex, Nika runs her fingers over the smooth nape of her customer's neck, thinking about what her aikido master has taught her. She could break this customer's neck if she wanted to. It happens to be a woman but it could just as easily be a man. A sudden, seemingly effortless twist, like you see in martial arts movies. You keep your hands open: it's all in the wrists. They don't teach that move to everyone. Her aikido master says she's the best student he ever had, a true artist.

The move has its advantages and disadvantages. You have to be up close, practically on intimate terms with the victim in order to use it on them: standing behind them, like the customer, or beside them, like Mary Ann snipping idly with her scissors as she doles out unwanted advice. Over a cup of coffee with Mary Ann that morning, Nika made the mistake of confiding the feelings aroused by her father's revelations: despair at realizing that her life had been full of unnecessary suffering, anger at both her parents and her brother, who seemed to have avoided any contagion. Mary Ann evidently viewed this disclosure as a kind of empowerment, authorizing her to launch an intervention.

July 4

Going to stay home sweltering for the holiday. Got to finish the story for tomorrow night. I'll sit here all night if I have to. Idea for title: "The Muse of Violence."

It's rush hour and the populace has poured into the streets like a mob escaping from a fire. Nika has agreed to one last meeting with Mario's manager, in front of a Starbucks on Fourteenth Street. At exactly five o'clock the melancholy manager is coughed up by the throng. The two exchange curt greetings and stand with their backs to the Starbucks window, inches away from a row of glassy-eyed coffee drinkers who pretend not to see them.

What is Mario hiding? Nika demands. Lack of artistic talent?

No, he can paint like Leonardo da Vinci if he wants to.

Why does he send his manager out to ask for a date?

I'm his manager. I manage things.

The crowd surges in front of them like a torrent. Nika thinks: You only get one chance to jump in and be carried away. The manager eyes her nervously.

So would you call Mario? Here's his cell number.

He hands her a business card with Mario's cell number on it.

OK, she says. I'll think about it.

She dives into the crowd, thinking about it. There's more to this Mario than meets the eye, she decides. He's a weirdo at best, at worst a serial killer. Is he planning to kill me? Get me to pose nude and strangle me with electrical tape? What he probably doesn't realize is that I could break his neck without missing a beat if he gave me a little inspiration. I'm an artist too, freezing random events in time and space, and he could be my muse instead of the other way around. Picture the scene in his studio: I'm perched nude on a high wooden stool, my face turned away, affecting a sensuous, self-absorbed expression as he sketches me. He slinks behind me with his electrical tape. Faster than thought, before he can slip the tape around my throat, I have one hand on his jaw, the other behind his head and snap! just like that, he goes down staring in disbelief. It would be self defense—or better yet, the perfect crime. No one would even know I was there.

This heat is making people do crazy things.

July 5   A.M.

I've got to read tonight. Try to get this finished, type up the rest at work.

At home in her apartment Nika broods on what her brother has said. Maybe he's right: maybe she should forgive and forget, move on with her life. Is she trapped in some stupid neurosis, some rat race of compulsive re-enactment she isn't even aware of? It's ironic: when she thinks about forgiving her mother, she can't help remembering all those years of coldness and meanness and hostility, but what infuriates her most is her mother's deathbed conversion to decency and kindliness and little-old-ladyhood. Everyone seems completely taken in by it. The nurses at the hospice, Freddy, her father, even the cynical Mr. Salvucci—they all think she's the sweetest old lady who ever lived. How could Nika join their craven ranks? By refusing, she's putting a stake in the ground, standing up for the truth. A pardon would only make her complicit in her mother's crimes.

But as she's falling asleep, a thought takes shape in Nika's mind: Forgiveness is a two-way street. She can forgive if her mother can accept her forgiveness. And when she wakes up at 7:00 the next morning she feels cool and clear headed and a hundred pounds lighter. She knows she can forgive—she feels as if she has already forgiven—because she is sure her mother will accept her forgiveness, and that acceptance will represent an acknowledgement, even if unspoken, that she has something to forgive. She showers, bolts down her breakfast and hurries to the hospice, stopping at a florist to pick up a potted geranium, Mother's favorite flower.

When she arrives at the hospice she skitters past the receptionist and down the hall to her mother's room. Her mother's bed is empty and the room has been cleaned out.

"I'm so sorry," says the nurse, padding up behind her. "Your mother passed away during the night."

Note: Go back and give fictional names to Freddy and Mr. Salvucci. This is just a story, not real life, which is bad enough. Mom hasn't died yet. But when she does it will probably be like this—in the middle of the night, with no forgiveness and no reconciliation. A saint.

15

Continuation by Will Schaefer

Tuesday night's meeting began as a continuation of Brian's funeral, with crying by the women, long faces on the men, and a general atmosphere of sadness and impending doom. It was Sara's turn to read, and her story, as it turned out, was consistent with the overall mood. I dreaded seeing Eleanor and was hoping she'd skip the meeting. But she was the first to arrive, the same as always, a little self-conscious and shy but with a new tinge of sadness in her hard gray eyes. Kate and Josh arrived a few minutes later and I couldn't tell whether they perceived Eleanor any differently than before.

Sara slipped in while I was mixing up some lemonade in the kitchen. "How was *Lucia?*" I asked her.

"*Lucia?*" she smiled.

"*Lucia di Lammermoor.* Isn't that the opera you saw the other night?"

"Oh, it was great." She reached out to take her lemonade. "Especially the mad scene."

We observed a moment of silence, as we had for Jackie, only this time no one made any jokes about it. "The group's going to be a lot different without Brian," Eleanor said grimly.

"It sure is," Kate agreed.

I took a sip of my lemonade. "Do you think we should recruit some more members?"

"No," Josh blurted. "Not yet anyway. It seems too soon."

"I agree," said Kate. "The five of us have got to work this through together."

"I assume everyone wants to stay with the group?"

"Absolutely," Kate said. "It's all the more important now because of what's happened."

"We're like survivors of a disaster," Eleanor added. "We have to stick together and we have to go on with our work."

"Writing is a demanding profession," Sara said, nodding solemnly, and the others seemed to agree. "You can't run away from it no matter how much you want to."

Josh bowed his head, as he had done during the moment of silence. "Literature takes no prisoners."

"On the contrary," I said, downing the rest of my lemonade. "It seems to have captured us all."

After a few more preliminaries, which did nothing to lighten our mood, everyone settled into their seats and Sara began to read her story, entitled "The Muse of Violence." It was the story of a bored, narcissistic young woman much like Sara, only her name is Nika and she works cutting hair at a unisex hair salon in Tribeca. Her best friend is Mary Ann, a 37-year-old redhead who stands beside her all day dishing out stupid advice. One of Nika's regulars at the unisex shop is Mario Migliori, an artist who seems to enjoy the sensation of her fingers brushing against his neck. His manager, Steve Tennenbaum, explains that Mario needs a muse in order to go on with his work. Nika is preoccupied with her estranged mother who is dying of cancer. She spends her spare time studying aikido; her aikido master has taught her a forbidden move, a move that could be used to break a man's neck. She wonders if Mario is really an artist or a serial killer trying to lure her into his clutches. What Mario doesn't realize is that she could break his neck if he gave her a little inspiration.

When her mother dies without any reconciliation, Nika falls into deep existential despair. She doesn't feel devastated or sad or even relieved, the way you're supposed to feel when your mother dies of cancer. Instead she feels heavy and thick-headed and above all angry at her mother for dying before she could forgive her and she could accept her forgiveness. She can never experience the purification that comes from forgiveness, even unacknowledged forgiveness— and now, as her brother warned her, it's too late. In an instant her heart has clogged with a lifetime supply of bitterness that she will never be rid of.

She walks around at random for an hour or two, stopping occasionally to examine her lethal hands, which feel cold in spite of the summer heat. She sits down on a bench in Battery Park in the blinding sun and dials Mario's number on her cell phone. *Who will make the first move?* she wonders. *Either way, the denouement will be swift, painless, astonishing.*

"Nika!" He's excited, a little flustered, though he seems to be expecting her. "So glad you called!"

"I'm ready when you are."

"OK. I'm ready. Where would you like to meet?"

"Someplace private. I don't want to lose my job."

"How about my studio?" he says. "No one will ever know you were here."

"Perfect," she says, her cold hands tingling. *"That would be perfect."*

We were all left speechless by Sara's story. After what we'd been through in the past few weeks, her detached, monotonous reading took on an oracular quality, as if she were giving us a glimpse into the future. We listened anxiously, hoping—or dreading—to hear clues to our fates. And it would have been hard not to see ourselves reflected in the characters. Kindly, soft-spoken Eleanor was obviously Nika's hated mother. Mary Ann, the redheaded loser, could only have been Kate. Steve Tennenbaum, morose and sweltering in his black suit, was an almost photographic rendering of Josh. And I, who until then had escaped the grasping claws of fiction, had been assigned the ambiguous role of Mario Migliori, the aleatoric minimalist. Did Sara view me as a stalker, an artistic fraud who used others to pursue his dubious ends—and whose neck, if he stuck it out too far, she would snap in two? The depths of hostility in her story were astonishing, like the unexcavated strata of some ancient city repeatedly brought down by violence.

"Well," Eleanor finally said. "You certainly covered all the bases. Adultery, child abuse, betrayal, inspiration, forgiveness, violence, possibly murder. What are you going to do for an encore?"

"I was thinking of something along the lines of Harry Potter," Sara deadpanned.

"The characters are fantastic," Josh said. "I really identified with Steve Tennenbaum."

I wanted to ask him: Do you identify with your own face when you see it in the mirror? But I limited myself to one incredulous snort, which I immediately concealed in a coughing fit.

"And the others," Josh went on, less innocently. "For example, Nika's so-called best friend Mary Ann." He glanced at Kate and then swung his dark eyes back toward Sara. "No offense, but she totally reminded me of Kate. That's who you had in mind, wasn't it, Sara?"

Sara smiled. "Resemblance of the characters to any person is entirely coincidental."

"Any person living or dead," Eleanor murmured.

Kate had been seething at Josh's remarks. Now she glared at Eleanor with a scowl that might have reflected either fury or alarm. "What do you mean?"

"The phrase is supposed to be, 'resemblance to any person living or dead,'" Eleanor explained. "That's what it always says if you look at the disclaimer on the back of a title page."

Kate's expression made it clear that she had nothing but contempt for Eleanor. But rather than waste her hostility on another woman, she turned it back toward Josh. "For me," she said, boring her eyes into his, "the story perfectly captures the moral vacuousness of a paternalistic society. The lack of commitment to any real values and how this corrodes the relationships between women. The consequent loss of faith in women's ability to understand what's happening in their lives."

Josh smiled tentatively, like Steve Tennenbaum in the story. Sara rescued him, nodding at Kate as if she were humoring a child. "Did you agree with Mary Ann that Nika should tell her mother that her father had been cheating on her all his life?"

"Yes, I did," Kate said firmly. "I think her mother had a right to know that before she died."

Eleanor leaned forward and cleared her throat. "Maybe Nika did the right thing in not telling her," she suggested. "Maybe that's not the kind of thing you need to know on your deathbed. That and all the other stuff about how much everybody in the family hated her. She didn't need to hear that when she was dying of cancer."

Eleanor turned to Sara with a sudden urgency: "That's right, isn't it? Nika never told her mother she hated her, did she?"

"I don't think so," Sara said. "She thought it should have been obvious."

"You say Nika hates her mother," Eleanor pressed on, "but she visits her every day."

"It's an animal instinct," Sara said. "Nothing more. Nika is totally selfish, just like your daughter."

"My daughter?"

"I'm sorry," Sara blushed. "I meant Margaret's daughter in your story."

It was an awkward moment. Eleanor and Sara couldn't look at each other and I was afraid Kate would blurt out some accusation that would only make matters worse. And so I did what I usually do in such situations: I deflected the discussion back to the craft of writing. "I loved the detached psycho style of narration," I said, drawing Sara back into the group. "It's a perfect correlative to the mind of the main character. It's as if we're watching a slow-motion train wreck unfolding right before our eyes."

"Yeah," Josh nodded. "But the train wreck never quite happens."

"That's right. We're left hanging at the end, wondering what's going to happen next. Is Mario a blocked artist or a serial killer? Why does Nika walk into his trap? Is it because she wants him to kill her, or wants a chance to break his neck? Who makes the first move? Does one of them die in the end?"

Sara took a sip of her lemonade. "You'll have to wait for the sequel."

Before we adjourned that night I did something a little unusual. I read a story myself. It was one of those "autobiographical" stories that young writers like to spend their time on, recounting a difficult coming of age in a heartless, dysfunctional world.

The story was set in a small river town in southeast Missouri, near Cape Girardeau where I was born. It's not quite the Midwest, not quite the South, not even exactly part of the modern world. The river isn't anything Huck Finn would recognize, except during a flood. The rest of the time it's an enormous concrete-encased barge canal that children are ordered to stay away from. In other ways, life on the Mississippi hasn't changed much at all. There are still drunken fathers who beat their kids and preachers who try to put the fear of God into them and charlatans of all stripes who succeed for a while in small ways before they move on to higher office. There's still racism and hypocrisy and a few people who can't pray a lie. All those things were in the story I read that night, but the reason I read it was to show that people can still get along in spite of it all. If a 17-year-old kid from southeastern Missouri who can't take the hypocrisy and abuse any longer can leave home and never go back and still find his way in the world, then our little group of sophisticated New Yorkers, in spite of their petty jealousies and misunderstandings and even the violent deaths of two of their friends, should be able to heal their wounds and overcome whatever force it was that was afflicting their lives. All it takes is honesty and love and patience and a little bit of luck. That's why I read the story that night and that's the message I hoped the group would take away from it.

In fiction everything can seem so simple.

16

Kate's body was fished out of the Hudson River the following evening by a NYPD patrol boat near the docks off West 35th street. Early the next morning I heard it on the news as I was eating breakfast and immediately called Sara on her cell phone. She sounded shaken but didn't seem to be crying.

"Listen," I said. "Can I come over? Or meet you somewhere? We need to talk."

"I guest this means I'm next," she said.

"What are you talking about?"

"It's always the last person who has read, isn't it?"

"Well—"

"It's like Scheherazade. You tell a story and then they kill you. I read Tuesday night and that means I'm next."

I felt a chill when she said that. "Not if we stop her."

There was a long pause before Sara spoke again. I could hear the TV or radio playing in the background. "How could Eleanor have done this? They found Kate's body in the river. You think Eleanor could have pushed her in?"

"It's got to be Eleanor. She's the only one who read her story and didn't get killed before the next meeting." That didn't sound very logical, or very reassuring either. "In any event," I went on, "this is way beyond coincidence. It's got to be someone in the group."

"I'm afraid you're right."

"Look, you can stay over here for a few days. I'll sleep on the couch."

"You don't have a couch."

"I'll get a couch."

"I can stay with my parents. I'll be OK."

"We have to talk to Detective Falcone. We have to tell him about Eleanor."

"I won't argue," Sara said. "I wish we'd talked to him sooner."

"I'll call him this morning. I just want to make sure you're all right."

"I'll be fine."

Sara's Journal
July 7

Last night they pulled Kate out of the river. Maybe it was cool in there at least. That makes three.

Everything seems to be unraveling. On TV they say the temperature's coming down but it never does and now nobody believes anything they say. The smiling meteorologists are totally unreliable. Is the government pressuring them to placate the masses with hope of relief?

Meursault in Camus's *The Stranger* kills a man for no reason except the noonday heat. Is that what they're afraid of, some kind of existential breakdown? Is this unbearable heat a good enough motive for killing people?

Continuation by Will Schaefer

I hurried to the office and spent an hour clearing my inbox of the morning's clutter before I could even think about calling Falcone. There was already a news story on the internet about Kate's death and a funeral scheduled for Saturday afternoon on Staten Island. I asked Martin, who sat at his computer downloading songs for his iPod, to notify everyone in the group and to arrange for a nice flower arrangement to be sent in our names. "This is getting monotonous," he said. "What kind of refreshments are you serving at these meetings?"

"It's not a joke," I growled.

"It certainly isn't. I'm hoping that being your assistant isn't as dangerous as being one of your friends."

"Listen, Martin—"

"I'm sorry." With a few keystrokes he opened his writers' group file and deleted Kate's name and contact information as if she had never existed. "That means you're down to three, besides yourself." He glanced up slyly. "Is there any chance Helen could get into the group?"

I stalked away in disgust and locked myself in my office, upset about Kate but even more urgently worried about Sara. Although I'd thought it best to squelch the Scheherazade theme, it was true that the murders seemed to follow the readings. The pattern seemed obvious, but I kept telling myself that it could have all been a coincidence. I couldn't bring myself to think the unthinkable: that this madness would continue and Sara would be the next victim.

Before I could untangle my thoughts, Martin knocked on the door with an urgent message. "There's a Detective Falcone on the phone who says he needs to speak to you immediately."

Rather than talk on the phone, we agreed to meet at a Starbucks near Grand Central Station. Falcone was working undercover, wearing a Yankees hat with the beak turned down, and he paid no attention when I walked into the shop. I ordered coffee and a danish and found a space beside him at the counter that overlooked the window, where he stood spreading butter on a bagel, half-crouched with one of his feet on the foot rail like a baseball manager perched on the dugout steps. His eyes seldom met mine, but when they did I felt like a relief pitcher blowing the seventh game of the World Series.

He spent an inordinate amount of time buttering his bagel and stirring the sugar and cream into his coffee, as if to emphasize that he had all the time in the world. I slurped my coffee anxiously as he aimed his languid gaze at an attractive woman passing by on the sidewalk.

"I'm glad you called, Detective," I said, preparing to give him the goods on Eleanor. "I was just getting ready to call you. You see—"

"Forget it," he interrupted.

"No, I need to—"

"I do the talking. Okay?"

"Okay."

"There's a school of thought in the Department," he said without turning towards me, "that I ought to bring you in."

"Me? Why me?"

He took a bite of his bagel and chewed it carefully. "You're the common thread, aren't you? All three of them were in your writing group."

"That doesn't prove anything."

It was the wrong thing to say. I could see his eyebrows twitching upwards.

"Look, this is absurd," I pleaded. "These people were my friends, and if you'd only listen to me—"

"I'm sure you're aware that most murderers know their victims."

"So the fact that they were my friends counts against me. Is that it?"

He shrugged and took a long sip of his coffee. "There are friends and there are friends, you know what I mean?"

A piece of danish caught in my throat and I washed it down with a quick slurp of coffee. "Not really."

"Some friends are closer than others, that's all." He smirked into his coffee. "And if they write stories about each other, that's even closer, right?"

"It could be."

"You write stories about people, who knows what could happen?"

I took another sip, trying to keep my hand from shaking, but before I could answer he cut me off. "Anyway"—finally he turned to face me—"I've decided not to take you in. But I am going to keep an eye on you."

"Be my guest."

"Maybe both eyes."

"You can watch me day and night for all I care. In fact I wish you would. I'm a potential victim too, you know."

"The Department can't be responsible for your safety." He returned to his bagel, temporarily focusing his surveillance on an Asian beauty who stood at the curb waving for a cab.

"No, I'm sure you can't."

"Personally, I don't think you did it," he said. "But like I say, not everybody in the Department agrees. You know how it is, with the media playing it up. There's a lot of pressure to make an arrest."

"Yeah, I'm sure that's true. And in fact—"

"So what I need to know is whether you're willing to cooperate."

"Sure, I'll cooperate. I'm trying to cooperate right now. I'm trying to tell you who did it, if you'd only let me."

Suddenly Falcone seemed to have had his fill. He slipped off the stool and swept the rest of his food into the trash bin before I knew what was happening.

"What do you want me to do?" I pleaded.

"I'll give you a week," he said.

"A week to do what? A week to get killed?"

He bent closer, boring his eyes into mine. "For now, just keep doing what you've been doing. Whoever the killer is— assuming it's not you—we don't want to alarm them."

17

My meeting with Detective Falcone left me so shaken that I had to stop for a quick drink on my way back to work. Everyone plays the crime lottery in New York: when you get up in the morning you know that in the random collisions of eight million lives you may become a victim or a suspect or both. But to be told by the police that you're a suspect in three murders and at the same time that you should "keep doing what you've been doing"—in other words, that you'll be arrested unless you allow yourself to be used as bait for the real killer—was a new and unnerving experience. Up to then my mood had been surprisingly calm, as if whether to give Eleanor's story to the police was the biggest issue I faced. But now it was clear that Falcone had set his sights on me and the other members of the group. I was being watched, we were all being watched, and whoever didn't get killed was for that reason a prime suspect. What did he mean, he would give me a week? I remembered what Sara had said: if the police don't have the evidence, they always manage to find it somehow.

And I had my own secret reasons for being worried. It was obvious that Falcone had read the victims' stories, or at least some of them, and in those stories he might have thought he'd found the killer's motive. "There are friends and there are friends"—I shuddered when he said that, because it could mean only one thing. He had read Jackie's amorous memoirs and discovered that I was one of the characters.

Not long after she joined the group, Jackie and I enjoyed a one-night stand—actually less than one night, more like a couple of hours—on a Thursday evening when she was supposed to be working late at the office. It was a harmless enough entertainment, yet I immediately regretted it, and I made her swear that she wouldn't write up a play-by-play and bring it to the next meeting. That would have exposed me as a hypocrite and ended any chance I had with Sara. I tried to get Jackie to promise that she wouldn't write about it at all, but she just giggled and insisted she could do whatever she wanted in the privacy of her own home. I was angry at her flippancy and at myself for giving her that kind of power over me. I wouldn't be surprised if that incident found its way into one of her stories.

There you have it, Detective Falcone. I made love to the victim, I even got mad at her, but I didn't kill her. She was a funny and good-hearted woman under her shell of sarcasm and I miss her. Is that the sort of confession you were looking for? If you need more, don't forget about Kate, who thought every man was a rapist. What kind of stories did she write about me?

When I returned to work I had another unnerving experience. As I stepped into my office I found Martin rifling through my desk drawers, pulling out files and stuffing them into a cardboard carton. "Just catching up on my filing," he muttered, suddenly reversing directions.

I snatched the carton and inspected the files before he could shove them back into the drawer. They were mostly of a personal nature: my resume, notifications about my compensation and benefits, some press releases I had written and some of my files about the writers' group.

"What are you doing with this stuff?" I demanded.

"I'm just trying to put your files in some kind of order," he said. "Would you be happier if I sat around polishing my nails like Helen?"

"Yes, please do."

"You're so paranoid."

Martin was right. From that day forward I lived my life against an accelerating drumbeat of fear and paranoia. When I walked down a street, especially at night, I kept a close watch on passing vehicles and an even closer watch on those that seemed to be lingering behind or ahead of me for no apparent reason: taxis, vans, panel trucks—any of them, for all I knew, might harbor a murderer like the hit-and-run driver who killed Brian or a team of cops gathering evidence to use against me.   And beyond such mundane fears, Detective Falcone had stirred my greatest dread, the fear of exposure I had carried with me from childhood: the certainty that sooner or later the truth would come out and I'd be exposed as a fraud.   Sara said my biggest problem was that I was always hiding something, and that was truer than she realized.   I had secrets I didn't even want to admit to myself, let alone to anyone else.   If my little fling with Jackie came to light, everyone in the writers' group would know I was a hypocrite, using the group as a way to meet women, having sex with them and pretending nothing had happened, even to the extreme of concealing my relationship with Jackie after she was murdered. And in that event I could forget about ever seeing Sara again.

Before I left work that evening, I dug out all my personal files and my papers relating to the writers' group—including copies of the stories I'd read to the group—and walked them down to the shredder, where I fed them in and watched them squiggle into oblivion. Of course I had no way of knowing what Martin had already copied, but if he was leaking documents to Falcone I wanted to make sure their collaboration was over. A quick search of Martin's desk turned up nothing of an unusual or suspicious nature, except a carton full of spread sheets and other financial records that meant nothing to me at the time.

When I left for the day I walked ten blocks out of my way and stood under an awning across the street from Sara's office building, wondering when she would be coming out and where she would go after work. Then I glimpsed her swinging through the revolving door and into the crowd that flowed toward Fifth Avenue. It was easy enough to follow her without being seen: unlike me, she had no reason to think she was being followed. She stayed with the crowd for a couple of blocks and then cut east to Second Avenue, where I almost lost her as she stepped around a corner and disappeared into a narrow doorway. When I looked at the sign over the door I understood where she had gone: Kim's Academy of Martial Arts, offering lessons in karate, tae kwan do, and other ways of turning your hands into lethal weapons. Like Nika in her story, Sara had apparently stopped for some deadly guidance from her master on the way home from work. I bought a *New York Post* and found an inconspicuous place to stand in a doorway across the street. When I thought about what might happen if Sara caught me following her, I felt a little tightening around my neck.

I was worried about Sara, but not too worried to have indulged in a little internet research at her expense. A Google search that afternoon had turned up a listing of all the operas playing in New York within the past month. As I suspected, *Lucia di Lammermoor* was not among them. That confirmed Dr. G's conclusion that Sara had lied to me about her reason for not accepting my dinner invitation. Google taught me a couple of other things about Sara. There wasn't any surgeon in New York or New Jersey with her last name who could have been her father, and no family with that name in the New Jersey town she claimed to have grown up in. I located a Yale graduate with her name and approximate age, but the alumni directory placed her family's address in the Bronx, a borough not noted for its country clubs or private schools. I had the sinking feeling that some of my other illusions about Sara were about to be shattered. I couldn't forget those early stories she'd showed me when she joined the group, so classic in their spare beauty and humanity. That was the real Sara, I told myself, not the nihilistic Nika of her recent work. But then why was she avoiding me and lying to me?

After about an hour she emerged from the doorway and headed uptown, presumably en route to her apartment on the Upper West Side. But at the corner of 59th and Lexington she jumped on a bus that was headed in the opposite direction. There was no way I could have squeezed onto that bus, crowded as it was, without being noticed, so I hung back until it had lumbered away and motioned for a cab. Luckily the cab I hailed was a real cab and not one of the undercover police cars painted to look like yellow cabs that had been tailing me all night. The driver was a young man from some African country where evidently it's considered impolite to break eye contact with the person you're talking to, even when you're driving and that person is sitting in the back seat.

"Follow that bus," I told him, hoping it would at least force him to look through the windshield.

His eyes widened in disbelief as well as appreciation for the bulletproof shield that separated us. "The bus? Follow the bus?"

"Yes. I want you to follow that bus. Just stay about half a block behind it."

"If you want to take the bus I will stop so you can get on it. It only costs two dollars."

"I don't like buses," I said. "That's why I take cabs. Do you know where that bus goes?"

"It goes to Queens."

"Good. Then let's go to Queens. But I don't want to get there any sooner than it does."

Creeping along behind the bus, we made slow progress down 59th Street, pausing every two blocks to let the bus absorb a few more passengers. Then we followed it onto the Queensboro Bridge and sped past Roosevelt Island into Queens. The bus slowed down again and fifteen minutes later, somewhere along Queens Boulevard, I saw Sara hop down and step purposefully toward my cab. "Quick, go around the bus," I told the driver. "And then stop and let me off as soon as you can."

By the time I hit the sidewalk, having placated the driver with a generous tip, Sara had almost disappeared from sight as she bobbed along in the crowd drifting down Queens Boulevard. I hurried behind her until she slipped through the doorway of a large, seedy-looking structure called "St.

Katherine's Health Center" that turned out to be a nursing home for indigent cancer patients. I learned what I needed to know a few seconds later when I stepped up to the reception desk.

"I'm with the woman who just walked in," I told the nurse.

"She's with her mother," the nurse told me. "Do you want me to tell her you're here?"

"No, that's okay," I said. "I'll wait outside."

Sara's Journal
July 7

Tonight when I left aikido I had the feeling I was being stalked. Just one of those times you feel a pair of unwelcome eyes following you. When I turned around I saw a guy duck into a store about a block behind me. I hate to say it but he looked a lot like Will. Am I getting paranoid? Luckily I was able to jump on the bus to Queens before he saw where I was going.

Mom gets worse every day. I can't stand to be in the room with her when Dad is there. He acts so sympathetic but I know he just wants her to die.

18

Continuation by Will Schaefer

The next morning I overslept, weighed down by grief, worry and suspicion. My thoughts swirled with replays of recent events: Kate's violent death, my encounter with Detective Falcone, and most of all my discovery of Sara's deceptions, which added an odd piquancy to my worries about her safety. No one in the group was safe, and no one could be trusted, not even Sara—that last thought both troubled and comforted me, balancing my fear of exposure with the hope of moral equivalence. I desperately wanted to believe I still had a chance with Sara, and that she was worthy of my trust even if I was unworthy of hers. Yet nothing was what it seemed: victims were suspects, suspects victims; my assistant, instead of assisting, was spying for the police. Zunax itself was like a dinosaur wading cheerfully into a bog.

I arrived at the office an hour late—it was Friday and the building was already like a ghost town. Everyone had decided to stretch the weekend into three days, four days, a week at the beach. Most of the senior management were in the Hamptons or had fled to uncharted territory beyond the range of their smartphones. Milton Babst, I'd heard, was spending his vacation at a lamasery in Nepal, where he hoped to find inspiration for a profitable third quarter. Presumably Bob Tedder had escaped to some love nest with Julie Kim, since they'd both vanished around the same time. Their secretaries insisted they were attending a business meeting in San Diego, but no one else in the department had heard of such a meeting. For a man who in every other respect was so secretive and self-protective, Bob Tedder was hard to fathom when it came to his relationship with Julie Kim. It was almost as though he didn't care whether he got caught.

"Obviously he's got pictures," Martin suggested.

"They must be pretty good ones," I said.

"Milton Babst with a goat. And I don't mean Mrs. Babst."

I had no tolerance for small talk with Martin after his attempted espionage of the day before. I kept a sharp eye on him and was relieved to see him preoccupied with hauling boxes of spread sheets in and out of the file room—a "special corporate project" that someone in Finance had assigned him, which thankfully had nothing to do with me. Having satisfied myself that my files were safe, I tried to forget my troubles by immersing myself in my work.

As usual, before I could do any work I had to spend a couple of hours checking emails. In the past few months the number of email messages had grown exponentially—in February there had been fifty a day and now in July I was receiving four hundred, all from within the company—and the importance of each message had diminished at the same rate, with the result that by year end the average Zunax employee would spend his entire work day reading and responding to internal email messages that had nothing to do with his job. On that particular morning I deleted five emails about menu changes in the cafeteria, six about the renovation of the gym, and seven about funeral arrangements for the mother-in-law of a secretary in the San Francisco office who had passed away at the age of 92. On a brighter note there were birthday greetings for five employees, none of whom I knew, though I appreciated being invited to join them for cake and ice cream, bagels, pretzels, and a chocolate fondue fountain. My inbox contained important announcements about the day care center, the credit union, flu vaccinations, pension rights, the 401(k) plan, stock options, the United Way campaign, the blood drive, the women's network, the diversity program, the political action committee, the privacy policy, insurance benefits, vacation arrangements, sick days, personal time, telephone coverage, working from home, mandatory training, financial planning, software upgrades, fire drills, emergency services and job safety. There were emails addressed to me (almost always from someone I didn't want to hear from), emails on which I was copied (which meant the message wasn't really for me but I had to read it anyway), reply-all responses from the other recipients (including those who didn't need to receive the original message), and successive rounds of reply-all responses to the earlier responses from those who never should have been copied in the first place—the totality of which, before the chain reaction ended, ran into hundreds of messages. And to top it off there were a dozen emails from Information Technology notifying me that pornographic spam from outside the company had been intercepted on its way to my computer, and providing an itemized list of each blocked message complete with URL accompanied by a warning that opening such messages would be a violation of company policy which could lead to disciplinary action up to and including termination.

At last, after I'd spent two hours opening and deleting all these emails, I came across an urgent message from Bob Tedder, sent via iPhone from an undisclosed location. He was forwarding an inquiry from the head of Investor Relations about bouncing vendor checks. When I saw who the message came from I didn't even have to read it. Bob's messages always consisted of the same two words: "Please handle."

It seemed that bills from various suppliers—quite a few of them, actually—had gone unpaid, and a number of large checks had bounced. A supplier in Germany posted an angry bulletin on its website accusing Zunax of fraud and warning others not to accept the company's checks. Now the stock analysts were starting to ask questions, and "Please handle" meant that I was supposed to come up with an answer. Like Lindsay Lohan on a bender, the situation could get ugly fast.

I took the elevator down to the fifteenth floor, an enormous hive of cubicles that was the seat of Finance. Searching for the queen bee—Luella Borgia, our recently-appointed CFO—I passed row after row of cubicles buzzing with accounting drones glued to their computer screens. Luella was out of the office, along with all the other higher-ups, leaving one Elizabeth Grady, a youngish accounting manager who seemed ready to tear out her straggly brown hair, in charge of the department. "We're incredibly busy, as you can see," she explained, with a gesture encompassing the vast floor of humming cubicles. "A few payments must have slipped through the cracks."

"Just a temporary glitch?"

"It's being fixed as we speak."

Bean counters, Babst had called them, in a tone of contempt. As I navigated my way back to the elevator I peeked into one of the cubicles and found myself confronted by a very attractive young Hispanic woman whose computer

screen sparkled with on-line salsa lessons provided by the
Employee Development department.

"How many beans can a bean counter count?" I asked
foolishly.

"Just catching up on my emails," she smiled.

I admit I didn't give a lot of thought to the press release I
wrote about the payment problems. If I had it to do over
again, I would have made the CFO sign off on it. But she
was at some meeting in Switzerland, or so they told me, and
the analysts couldn't wait another day for an explanation. I
wrote what I thought was the truth and frankly I had no idea
the subject was particularly important. The truth is, if I had it
to do over again I probably would do the same thing.

Before he left for lunch, Martin gave me the latest scoop
on Paul Gratzky. "There's a rumor that he's been
hospitalized."

"Is he sick?"

"Nervous collapse, whatever that is. Either it's part of
the scam or he's finally starting to have some of his own bad
luck."

"What about the hedge fund?"

"It's just a bunch of supercomputers talking to each
other, isn't it?" Martin chuckled. "Probably runs itself."

I didn't see anyone I knew in the cafeteria, so I brought a
tuna salad sandwich back to my desk and ate by myself,
feeding my anxiety and a growing sense of impending doom.
I wanted to see Sara, wanted to confront her with her lies and
tell her in the same breath that they meant nothing to me—

but I was ashamed of my own deceit in tracking down the truth about her. The longer I pretended not to know what I knew, the more deceitful and treacherous I would seem when the reckoning finally came. And of course I was terrified that my other deceptions would be exposed. In every part of my life I was walking a tightrope between fear and guilt, truth and fiction, love and hate, possibly life and death. As I walked that tightrope there was always something following me, a police van or a yellow cab or my own bloodshot conscience, taking careful aim, observing every move and every hesitation, recording every glance over the shoulder. I knew I couldn't bear this state of suspended panic much longer. Whatever was going to happen would just have to happen.

I picked up the phone and dialed Sara's cell number.

We met after work at a bar on West 55th Street called Sparrow, which was almost too crowded to carry on the kind of conversation we needed to have. We sat at the bar sipping margaritas, our heads close together in a kind of conspiratorial intimacy as I briefed her on my encounter with Detective Falcone (minus his hints about my affair with Jackie) and lamented the fact that she and I were being used as decoys to flush out the murderer.

"I'm worried about you," I said, leaning so close that her hair brushed my face. "I don't want you to get hurt."

"I can take care of myself," she laughed, twisting away from me. "Remember Nika in my story? The woman with the lethal hands?"

"How could I forget her?"

"That's me." She reached down and seized my wrist in what can only be described as a viselike grip and set her jaw as if she were about to hurl me into the outer boroughs. I thought of the Aikido academy and of poor Mario Migliori in her story, who may have had his neck snapped for the crime of asking her out. "If Eleanor gets within two feet of me I can break her neck."

"What if she runs you down with a car like she did Brian?" I pried her hand off my wrist and moved it out of her reach.

"I'll jump out of the way."

"Listen, Sara. It might be Eleanor or it might be someone else. You need to be careful. Can't you go stay with your parents in New Jersey for a few days?"

"Ordinarily I could," she lied—I wasn't supposed to know that her mother lived in shabby nursing home in Queens—"but they just left on a vacation to Italy."

"You could stay in their house, couldn't you? You need to get out of the city. Or you could stay at my place."

"I'll think about it. But what about you? All your friends have been getting killed. Doesn't that make you nervous?"

"I'm beyond nervous. I'm scared out of my wits."

"They were special friends, too."

"What do you mean?"

She swiveled on her barstool so she could face me directly. "Well, the people in the group aren't just casual acquaintances, are they?"

I tried to hide my alarm. "Have you talked to Detective Falcone?

"No? Why do you ask?"

"Just paranoid, I guess."

She excused herself to use the ladies' room and while she was gone I ordered another pair of margaritas, asking myself how much longer this game of cat and mouse could continue. We were lying to each other—both of us seemed to know that—and even the most sympathetic observer would have to wonder whether this relationship was headed in the right direction. When she came back I used the opportunity to pursue a slightly different approach.

"I've been meaning to ask you," I said, "if you don't mind talking about your story: what did Nika have against Mario Migliori? Assuming he wasn't a serial killer."

She smiled mischievously. "That's a big assumption. Nika didn't know what he was, remember?"

"OK, she had a suspicion—"

"Except that as an artist he was a charlatan."

"Aleatoric minimalism."

"Right."

"So what did she have against him?"

"You don't know?"

"That he kept asking her out?"

She laughed. "Maybe that he had his manager stalking her the way you've been stalking me."

I didn't have to pretend to be shocked. "What are you talking about?"

"Last night when I left the Aikido academy a man who looked a lot like you followed me up Second Avenue."

"Well, it wasn't me. I wouldn't do that."

She smirked skeptically. "OK, let's talk about Mario Migliori. What did he want from Nika? He was so obsessed with her that he couldn't work. He wanted her to be his muse."

"For that she was willing to break his neck?"

"What could be more humiliating"—she tilted her head back, turned her glass upside down and let the last drops of her margarita trickle through the ice—"than playing the muse to a charlatan?"

Another mischievous smile, then a glance at her phone and a suddenly remembered appointment, and before I knew it Sara had wriggled off her barstool and out the door.

Sara's Journal
July 8

Will is upset about the way I portrayed him in the story. Have to admit I like making him squirm. That was a good line I made up in the ladies room: "What could be more humiliating than playing the muse to a charlatan?" His deepest fear is that somebody might find out the truth about him (I should talk!)

I think he might have been the one following me. He keeps trying to lure me to his apartment. Claims to be worried about me. As if I had anything to fear from Eleanor! Too bad my parents don't really live in New Jersey or I'd go there just to get away from him.

19

Continuation by Will Schaefer

Kate's funeral was the next day at a big Catholic church in Staten Island, a borough I had never visited before and have no intention of ever visiting again. Like Hell in the ancient classics, it can be reached only by ferry, and the people you meet there seem shadowy, bitter and anxious to tell you their life stories. The fact that it's an island took on an unexpected significance for our little group, which gathered outside the church before the service so we could all sit together. To my surprise, Howard had come over with Eleanor on the ferry; he must have skipped his weekend in Vermont, as Eleanor had for the second week in a row. Howard was his usual affable, slightly pompous self, shaking hands with Josh and me as if we were there for a spaghetti supper in the church basement. When Sara arrived he seemed a little less friendly, nodding a quick hello and then barging between Sara and Eleanor to lead the way inside.

"I feel like I'm on *Survivor*," Eleanor whispered as we slid into our pew.

"That's how we all feel," I agreed.

Sara smiled warily. "Just as long as it isn't *Ten Little Indians*."

Howard shot a chilly glance at Sara. Evidently he was the only one who caught the allusion. *Ten Little Indians* was the movie version of *And Then There Were None*, the Agatha

Christie book I'd found on the little table next to my door just after we learned of Jackie's death. I'd been meaning to ask them who had returned it. Sara was right: it was worse than *Survivor*. It takes place on an island, but instead of being voted off, the characters are all murdered, one by one, before the story ends.

"Are you the one who brought that book back?" I asked Sara, a little too loudly. A flinty-eyed old lady kneeling in the next pew shot me a decidedly un-Christian glance.

Sara hesitated. "Back where? I have a copy at home."

I turned toward Josh, who stared back at me in confusion. "I've been meaning to bring this up—"

But I stopped short before I finished my sentence. Sara had crossed herself and dropped to her knees, Eleanor and Howard sat with their eyes cast down, and I couldn't tell whether the old lady in front of me was praying or getting ready to strangle me with her rosary. When the priest stepped forward to intone his first prayer, the church—which was filled to capacity—fell into a respectful silence, punctuated only by muffled sobbing. Clearly this was not just any funeral but the funeral of a young woman who enjoyed the love and respect of a great number of people. Our dwindling writers' group formed the smallest contingent of mourners. There must have been three hundred people there—her parents, sisters and brothers, nieces, nephews, uncles and aunts, grandparents and godparents, all trying to deal with their loss as best they could. And there were scores of others, including a large contingent of militant feminists wearing "Take Back the Night" T-shirts and dozens of professional friends and colleagues, including many tearful women from the shelter where she worked, as well as a gang of tattooed Goths from the bar on the far West Side where

I'd met her that night. Even Zelda's orange hair could be seen spiking up in one of the front pews. I looked around anxiously for Detective Falcone but didn't spot him in the crowd.

I was surprised and touched that Kate's death had affected so many. They all seemed not only sad and miserable but somehow unreal, because it was so hard to believe they were really there for her funeral. All of them, that is, except the priest, who seemed to view the funeral as a festive occasion. In spite of all the evidence to the contrary, he was adamant in his insistence that Kate was still alive, and in a better place. Her family at least seemed to take some comfort in that assertion. But the feminists from Manhattan were not amused. They seemed to have the quaint notion that a woman who was bludgeoned and tossed into the river to drown should be regarded as dead.

Another issue Father McDonagh tried to lay to rest was the problem of evil. "It wasn't God who did this to Kate," he said in his homily. "God was not responsible for what happened to Kate. When evil comes into our lives, we have to remember that it does not come from God. Quite simply, it comes from the Devil. The Devil and his evil work are not abstract, old-fashioned ideas or childish fantasies for a Halloween party or a Stephen King movie. They are real, as real as the air we breathe, and like the air they surround us every moment of our lives, whispering temptations that only our faith in God can protect us from. And sometimes, because we have free will, they will succeed and bring great harm and even death to innocent people. But Kate is beyond all that now. Today she is with Lord Jesus Christ and the Blessed Virgin Mary and we needn't fear for her anymore. She is alive in Heaven. But here on earth, here in New York

City, we do need to fear for ourselves. We must fear the Devil every day of our lives. He still walks the streets of New York."

This last part of Father McDonagh's homily met with a better reception from the feminists, especially his use of the masculine pronoun for the Devil, and probably from those whose buildings had 24-hour doormen to keep Old Ned from wandering in from the street. But for the rest of us— especially the writers' group—it was a demoralizing finale to a depressing afternoon. To think that we had been victims, not of chance or a deranged killer, but of the Devil himself, was almost more than anyone could bear. On the trip back to Manhattan I found myself wondering how many people who took the Staten Island Ferry threw themselves overboard, and how many of those were returning from funerals presided over by Father McDonagh.

Not that you needed Father McDonagh to be depressed on that ferry. The rancid odors of another stultifying summer evening, the sickening rhythm of the waves, the implacable grinding of the engines, all told us we had not left death and evil behind on Staten Island. Before us rolled Manhattan, unreal city, its skyscrapers thrusting up from below sea level to dazzle us with the blaze of the setting sun. Beside us loomed the Statue of Liberty, her torch extinguished, her vision dimmed, wary in her old age of the promises she made in her youth. All of us were on that ferry, all that were left of us—Sara, Eleanor, Josh and I, as well as Howard—and though we were tired and hungry and no one really wanted to talk to anyone else, there was something I needed to say to the group. So just before the ferry landed in Manhattan I picked my way through the huddled masses of camera-toting tourists and asked everyone to gather in the front of the cabin.

They came sullenly, haltingly, averting their eyes. The outpouring of grief and sadness that overwhelmed us at the funeral had subsided, as we crossed on the ferry, into a vigil of fear and suspicion. We were all on our own now, each calculating the odds of his or her own survival against the near certainty that someone was trying to kill us. Eleanor was still the most likely suspect, but as she stood beside me steadying herself on the support rail she seemed dwarfed by the very enormity of the crimes. Could it be that someone— or something—else had been responsible for these deaths? Was there some other common thread that linked the group's members? Even before Kate's murder, the downfall of Paul Gratzky—and Martin's suggestion that I could be drawn into Gratzky's widening gyre of misfortune—had been preying on my mind.

"This is a difficult time for all of us," I said when they had assembled in the front of the cabin. "Everyone's upset and worried and suspicious, and who wouldn't be, with everything that's been happening?" They stared back at me expectantly—everyone but Josh, who seemed lost in his own thoughts. "There's something I think you should know about. Have you all been following the Gratzky case?"

They nodded and I went on: "Well, as everyone's heard by now, it seems that association with Paul Gratzky has been dangerous, or at least unlucky, for a lot of people. First his wife died, then two of his children, then several of his business associates—"

"What does that have to do with us?" Josh demanded, jumping into the conversation. I had never seen him so agitated.

I smiled in what I hoped was a reassuring fashion. "Probably nothing. But in the interest of full disclosure, I just wanted you all to know that I have some connection with Gratzky, and so does Howard." I glanced at Howard, who squinted back at me with a puzzled expression. "I guess you could say I'm a business associate. The CEO of my company, Milton Babst, is a good friend of Gratzky's and—"

"If he's such a good friend, why is he still alive?" Sara asked without smiling.

"Good question," I said. "So far he's one of the survivors."

"What's the connection between you and Gratzky?" Josh pursued.

"He's a major shareholder of Zunax and he's on our board of directors. I've worked on a couple of projects for him—philanthropic projects, not connected with his hedge fund. And Howard does consulting work for my company— that's how I met Eleanor. You're a fairly good friend of Gratzky's, aren't you, Howard?"

"What are you getting at?"

"Nothing very logical. Just that in light of what's happened to Jackie and Brian and Kate, I thought everyone should know this, and if anybody feels that—"

Eleanor raised her voice louder than I'd ever heard it before. "You think they got killed because of Paul Gratzky?"

"Eleanor, this is ridiculous!" Howard shook a pudgy forefinger in front of my face. "What are you saying? That there's some kind of bad karma that attaches to anyone who knows Paul Gratzky and it can spread to people who don't even know him? I've never heard anything so stupid in my life!"

He put his arm around Eleanor's shoulder and whisked her away before I could answer her question. They melted into the crowd that was gathering to disembark.

"I agree it's ridiculous," I called after them. "I just wanted to give everyone a chance to come to their own conclusions."

"This isn't as stupid as it sounds," Josh said in a low voice. He stood beside me with his eyes cast down, hands hidden in the pockets of his black suit.

"What do you mean?"

"I'm in insurance. You knew that, didn't you?"

"Sure, I know that. But—"

"Bad things tend to happen in clusters that no one can explain in terms of cause and effect. Call it karma if you like. But I think it's something else."

"What? What is it?"

He shoved a business card into my hand and closed my fingers around it with a solemn nod. "Give me a call and we can talk about it."

When I turned around, I realized that Sara was gone. She had slipped into the crowd without a backward glance.

Sara's Journal
July 9

Sometimes I think Will has read too many novels. This afternoon on the ferry coming back from Staten Island he came out with the idea that everybody's getting killed because of some association with Paul Gratzky. Karma, somebody called it.

I think it's more like what the priest was talking about. Evil. It's as real as the air we breathe. It surrounds us every minute of our lives. But it's not some impersonal force like karma. It's walking the streets. It looks like the rest of us.

Continuation by Will Schaefer

On shore it was another oppressive night, the kind that even in the absence of specific reasons for despair might make you feel like a character in a Russian novel. A new weather system had gradually wrapped itself around the city, smothering the air in its fervid embrace. I decided to walk from the Battery to my apartment in Chelsea, which I figured would take about an hour. A yellow cab, probably containing Detective Falcone or one of his men, crept along at a distance behind me, but I pushed it out of my mind—in New York there's always a yellow cab creeping along behind you if you look for it. The air was almost too heavy to breathe, and as I made my way uptown I struggled to keep from being suffocated by my own desperate thoughts. Our safe return from Staten Island was an achievement of sorts, I told myself, in terms of *And Then There Were None*. In the Agatha Christie book all ten characters who visit the island end up dead. Four of us had made it back alive from Staten Island—but no, we'd merely escaped from one island to an infinitely more treacherous one. In Manhattan they don't vote you off, they kill you. And it tortured me to think that the next victim could be Sara.

I carried that worry with me all the way uptown to my apartment—where a kindly Tennessean named Jack Daniel lulled me to sleep—and even into my dreams, where I saw Sara running for her life past crowds of indifferent mourners into the arms of a smiling Father McDonagh. Luckily I woke up before he began his sermon. Stumbling out of bed, I realized that it was 8:15 on Sunday morning. I was late for my appointment with Dr. G.

I jumped into my shorts and running shoes and raced down to 14th Street. By the time I reached Dr. G's little patch of city property, it was 8:45 and the doctor had given up on me. He straddled his suitcase immersed in a chess game with himself, observed by the usual group of spectators. When I landed on the crate across from him—gasping for breath from my run—he pointed to the rusty sign that announced his cancellation policy.

"Afraid I'm gonna have to charge you," he said, shaking his head. "Had to start without you."

"How am I doing?"

"You were whupping me a minute ago," he smiled. "But then you sort of fell to pieces." He dragged one of his rooks forward a space. "Checkmate."

I handed him a $20 bill. "I just need to talk to you."

His smile widened and he shook his head. "There seems to be a misunderstanding here," he said. "This here's a chess playing establishment, not a talking establishment. For $20 you get to lose a game of chess and while you're losing you can talk as much as you want. But for plain talking the rate is $50 an hour."

"OK, but—"

"In advance. And you already used up the first forty-five minutes."

"OK." I pulled out my wallet and shelled out another thirty dollars..

On the park bench there were murmurings from the spectators. The teenager in the snowshoe-sized basketball sneakers called out something about his 9:00 o'clock appointment.

"Talk fast," Dr. G said, cranking the timer. "You got fifteen minutes."

There was a lot to tell him and he had an opinion about everything: Sara's disturbing story and her even more disturbing life ("See, what'd I say about folks making up them stories?"), Kate's brutal death ("You could see that one coming a mile away!"), my encounter with Detective Falcone ("With the police, the last thing you ever want to do is know something"), and the anonymous phone calls that predicted each new murder ("Myself, I ain't worried—I got a unlisted number").

When the timer went off, I started to stand up and he grabbed my arm and pulled me down toward him. He spoke in a whisper, as if to keep the spectators from overhearing. "You need to worry more about Sara," he said, unsmiling. All the folksy good humor was gone.

"Why do you say that?"

"She just read her story, right?"

I nodded and leaned closer so I could hear what he was saying.

"Then you better keep your eye on her. She's next."

By 10:00 o'clock I was back at my apartment, showered, shaved and worried sick about Sara. I decided to call her as soon as I'd had breakfast and finished a few things I needed to do. For breakfast I dolloped a little Irish whiskey into a cup of coffee and topped it off with Redi-Whip to make sure it included all the essential food groups. Then I gathered all my files and papers relating to the writers' group, tore them into tiny pieces and hauled the pieces down the back stairs to the dumpster, observed only by Wolfgang, who snarled through Zelda's door every time I sneaked past her apartment with my plastic garbage bags.

When I came back upstairs the phone was ringing. Once, twice, three times—with a clench of fear I braced myself for the ring that would announce the next murder. And the fourth ring came, shattering my last shred of hope—who was the victim this time?—but before I could catch my breath the fifth ring came, and then the sixth and the seventh. I realized that this was just an ordinary phone call, the kind I used to get all the time. After all, it was eleven o'clock on Sunday morning, not the middle of the night. Not everybody I knew was a serial killer calling in death threats.

I grabbed for the phone. It was Sara and she was crying hysterically.

"I saw him. He's after me."

20

I hope I haven't given the impression that all the writers' group ever did was fight with each other. Until the night Jackie read her last story we had a pretty good time, laughing and joking and sugarcoating our criticisms with praise and encouragement, sometimes even experiencing flashes of literary illumination.

Just three weeks before Jackie's death we had a discussion that came back to me as I sat sipping my Irish coffee that Sunday morning after Kate's funeral. No doubt my recollection was triggered by Father McDonagh's words about the ubiquity of evil, but remembering it as I did gave me a little chill. It was the kind of chill you feel when you suddenly realize that whatever is or will be has been here all along.

Sara had read a story and I characterized her narrator—a young woman much like herself—as an unreliable narrator. Sara smiled a mischievous smile, proud yet a little embarrassed to have her irony so quickly exposed. But some of the others seemed to take my comment as an accusation.

"Unreliable?" Josh asked. "What do you mean?"

"An unreliable narrator is someone telling a story who isn't completely credible for one reason or another," I explained. "Maybe they're biased in some way, or they're trying to justify their actions."

"Or they're hiding something," Eleanor suggested.

"That's right," I agreed.   "Or maybe they just don't understand the story they're trying to tell. That's the classic example: Ford Maddox Ford's *The Good Soldier*, where the narrator spins out this long tale about his best friend and it's obvious to the reader and everybody else—but not to the narrator—that the friend has been sleeping with the narrator's wife all along. The whole effect of the book turns on that irony."

Did Eleanor blush when I said that?   That's what I seemed to recall as I thought back on it, but how much of that memory was prompted by what happened later? At the time I had no reason to attach any importance to Eleanor's reaction to what I'd said.

Jackie, for her part, jumped right into the discussion. "When you read a book it's like you're a detective," she said. "Or on a jury. You have to evaluate the credibility of the witnesses and decide for yourself what really happened."

"The tension is there in almost any book," I agreed. "Huck Finn doesn't really understand the issues he's dealing with. His abuse by his father, his relationship with Jim. The whole slavery issue and what it will lead to."

"So this is only when there's a first person narrator?" asked Josh.

"Not necessarily," Kate answered. "The most unreliable narrator of all is the omniscient third person who pretends to know everything like some patriarchal god. He—I'm sure it's a he—doesn't really know everything. But even if he did, he wouldn't reveal it to you because that would compromise his authority."

"Theologians have wrestled with the same problem," said Brian, as if he felt obliged to put in a word for the Man

Upstairs. "If God knows everything that's going to happen, why does it even have to happen?"

"Yeah," said Jackie, "why not just skip ahead to Judgment Day and find out how the story ends?"

We all enjoyed a laugh over that, and then Sara closed the loop with a characteristically insightful observation. "From the narrator's point of view," she said, "isn't there also such a thing as the unreliable reader?   Think of Meursault in Camus's *The Stranger.* He understands his story better than the reader ever will, because the reader can't help but cling to her own illusion that the universe must be intelligible."

"That's a great point," I said. "A similar variation—or I guess it's really a mirror image—is the guilty narrator. The narrator is telling the truth but the reader can't bring himself, or herself, to believe it. That's the technique in one of my favorite books, *The Talented Mr. Ripley.* The hero is a psychopath but you can't help identifying with him, even rooting for him, because he's cast in the role of the hero. And you justify this to yourself because you're sure he's going to get caught in the end."

"But he doesn't get caught, does he?" Josh frowned.

"No, he doesn't." They all glared back at me as if I were responsible for this perverse denouement. "And as a reader you're left with an unsettling combination of shame and elation"—

"Elation?"

"That's too strong a word." I felt like a heretic being questioned by the Spanish Inquisition. "It's not like I'm siding with the psychopath. But there's an emotion, call it sympathy or identification, that you feel for the hero even if he is a homicidal maniac."

Sara rescued me with her little ironic laugh. "It's a book about our complicity with evil."

21

Now Sara was on the phone gasping for breath as she struggled to describe the evil that was staring her in the face.

"I'm saw him. He's after me."

"Saw who? Who did you see?"

"He's after me. The guy that was stalking Kate."

I hesitated. What was she talking about?

"Don't you remember? When we were at Brian's funeral she said there was a man stalking her in a raincoat and a floppy hat?"

"Oh, right. I remember now."

"I saw him behind me, ducking in and out of doorways just the way Kate described him. I turned a corner and he followed me."

"Where are you?"

She was in the West Village, at the White Horse, where she'd gone to meet a friend for brunch. The friend—I assumed it was a woman—had called to cancel when Sara was about a block from the restaurant, leaving her at the mercy of the stalker, who had disappeared from view.

"Are you sure it's not just some street person?"

"I saw him, I tell you." Now she sounded angry at me. "The same guy Kate saw. He's wearing a raincoat and hat, just like she said, and carrying something in a bag."

"All right. Go on inside the restaurant. I'll be there in fifteen minutes."

It was a beautiful summer morning but in the interest of time I decided to take the subway. If a train came right away I could be at the White Horse in five minutes. I hurried down a urine-soaked staircase into the dreary netherworld of the Broadway IRT, a line constructed immediately after the invention of the wheel. On a Sunday morning in July the station had a steamy, Blade Runner quality that should have been warning enough to stay away. It was about a hundred degrees and the air smelled like ozone seeping out of a volcano. No train was in sight, and nobody waiting, but after a few minutes a screeching sound like fingernails on a blackboard announced the arrival of the Broadway Local. I found a seat amidst piles of discarded newspapers and tried to collect my thoughts. I was excited that Sara had called me, but worried about what I might be walking into. I glanced at my watch. With any luck I would be there in five minutes.

The doors clamped shut, followed by an encouraging wheeze, as if the air conditioner were working. This proved a false hope, as became clear when the train began to move. It lurched forward about fifty feet until it stood barely inside the tunnel, where it crept to an agonizing halt. After some huffing and puffing—which I concluded had to do with the brakes and not the air conditioning—it began to creak forward like an oxcart, and now when it stopped it actually moved backwards and repeated the same process in reverse. By this time I was dripping with sweat and ready to start screaming. When the torture had gone on for twenty minutes I did start screaming, regaling the empty car with an outburst of profanity that closely approximated my inner thoughts. In the middle of my tirade a homeless woman wobbled into the car to pick through the newspapers. She smiled knowingly, offering me the *New York Times Magazine* from one of her bags.

By the time I arrived at the White Horse, I had worked myself into a frenzy and Sara was nowhere to be found. The hostess, her suspicions aroused by my deranged, sweat-soaked appearance, refused to answer my questions and summoned the manager when I persisted. From the manager—a moonlighting mortician with wide-spaced eyes and a molded plastic smile—I learned that the restaurant, like a doctor's office or an insane asylum, could not divulge any information about the comings and goings of its guests, and that if I did not have a reservation, or could not state the name of the party under whose reservation I desired to be seated, I should immediately leave the premises or (this after five minutes of strenuous argumentation on my part, the use of profane language suggesting violence and sexual situations, and several references to the manager's mother) he would have no choice but to call the police. I pushed past him and stomped through the bar and the dining room—out of the corner of my eye I could see the manager dialing the police, but this was New York and I knew they'd never show up—until I had satisfied myself that Sara was nowhere on the premises. I had no way of knowing whether she had ever made it inside.

I fled across the street and stood on the corner, gazing in every direction in hopes of spotting Sara or her pursuer. I dialed her cell phone and got no answer. I called her home, her office; I even considered calling the police. While I stood immersed in these thoughts, a black SUV swerved out of the traffic on Hudson Street and almost ran me down. I jumped back and the car sped away before I could catch a glimpse of the driver. Was it the murderer? I wondered—trying for another "accident?" Or just a drunk who thought it was still Saturday night?

I knew Sara's address—she lived on West 104th Street, about a block from Broadway—though I'd never been to her apartment. Frankly, I wouldn't have gone to that address for Helen of Troy if the Broadway Local had been the only way to get there, but luckily there were alternatives: I could walk a couple of blocks to the C train or take a cab. Given the urgency, I decided to spring for a cab. The ride uptown was the usual near death experience—the driver's last job had been as a suicide bomber—and by the time I reached Sara's apartment I had almost forgotten the danger we were in. I stepped brazenly up to her building and let myself in without buzzing when one of the other tenants came out. Luckily there was no doorman, so I could jump on the elevator without being interrogated. Up to the fifth floor and down a dimly-lighted corridor—it was amazing how shabby the building was—I knocked on Sara's door and got no answer. Yet I thought I heard a TV or radio playing inside. I knocked harder and still got no answer.

I ran back downstairs in a frustrated frenzy and shuffled toward Central Park to collect my thoughts. Half a block down 104th Street I happened to glance behind me and then I saw him: the ungainly figure Sara had described, wobbling along behind me in floppy hat and raincoat, ducking hastily into a doorway the instant I turned around. Was he following me or sneaking back to Sara's apartment? I ran as fast as I could in that clinging, impenetrable humidity, dodging around old men with canes, young couples with strollers and a small swarm of teenage girls tapping text messages into their phones, until I came to a wary stop in front of the doorway where the stalker had disappeared from view. It was one of those steam-table cafeterias you find on the Upper West Side, where Latino countermen in white aprons scoop out beef brisket and stuffed cabbage to blue-haired old ladies and frail old men in sweat pants and sneakers, and there he was—or she, as it turned out: a pale, sticklike old woman in a beige raincoat large enough to withstand a tsunami and a floppy wide-brimmed hat that must have been designed to prevent skin cancer in the tropics, shuffling her way into the line and tottering unsteadily as she reached for her tray.

I suppose I should have been relieved, but the sight of that old lady only served to agitate me further. I hurried back to Sara's building and ran up the stairs to the fifth floor. At the end of the corridor, Sara's apartment door stood open. There were books and papers strewn all over the floor.

I took a step inside. "Sara! Sara! Are you here?"

There was no answer.

"Is anyone here?"

I ducked into the kitchen and pulled a French chef's knife out of a drawer before edging my way into the living room. The place looked like it had been ransacked.

"Sara?"

I hesitated before entering the bedroom, steeling myself for what I might find there. Slowly I pushed the bedroom door open and peered into the near darkness, groping around the corner for the light switch. The bed was a jumbled mess but there was no one in it. Clothes were piled on the chair and hanging from the knobs on the bureau. Nothing abnormal, except—and I didn't really notice it at the time—the lack of any family photos.

"What are you doing here?"

Sara stood behind me in the living room and I could tell she was angry. When I turned around with the knife in my hand she was also scared.

"Are you OK?" I asked her.

"What are you doing here?"

"I came up here because I couldn't find you."

"I asked you to meet me at the White Horse. I didn't ask you to break into my apartment with a knife in your hand."

"Sara—"

"What are you doing? Stalking me again?"

"Sara—"

"Put that knife down!"

It was not the best ten minutes Sara and I ever spent together. After laying the knife on a small table near the door, I explained what had happened on the subway and at the White Horse and how I came to her apartment and found it ransacked, demonstrating, to my own satisfaction if not to hers, that my intentions had been honorable and even heroic. She listened skeptically, keeping her distance, with her dark eyes darting between me and the knife as if she expected me to grab it again and finish her off.

"OK, why don't you go now?" she said when I had finished my explanation.

"Where were you?"

"I was taking my recycling down to the basement. Now please go."

"Sara, listen to me," I insisted. "Somebody came in here and ransacked your apartment."

"Maybe I'm in the middle of cleaning it. Sorry I didn't have it ready for your inspection."

"Somebody did this and it wasn't me."

"I'm glad to hear that. Now please go. I'm not having a good day."

I'm not having a good day. No, Sara, neither am I, between being desperately summoned to save you from the stalker, stranded on the subway from Hell, and racing heroically down 104th Street to confront a little old lady on her way to the early bird special, only to be driven from your apartment like a dog. I took the C train home and counted my blessings, which I could easily do on one hand with enough fingers left over to measure out a double Jack Daniel's in a slim glass loaded with ice cubes. As the afternoon wore on, my mood faded to black. Early that evening—the city was still running a high fever, over 100 degrees, with growing symptoms of hostility and disorientation—I left my apartment and wandered the streets for several hours, stopping at an occasional watering hole for a gulp of some suitably tropical drink. Mentally this trek was one long argument with myself. I wanted to jump back on the C train and take it back uptown. I wanted to stand in the bodega across the street from Sara's building and watch through the window until the owner threw me out, and if Sara came out her door I wanted to follow her wherever her mysterious purposes took her, even if it was somewhere I had no right to be. But I didn't do any of those things. The way she'd treated me that afternoon had struck a blow to my self-esteem. Whatever I was, I wasn't a stalker.

When I got back to my apartment I made the mistake of turning on the TV for the day's litany of murder and mayhem. Watching the news, you'd get the impression that the urge to violence is breathed into us by some outside force. There's racially-inspired violence, religiously-inspired violence, demonically-inspired violence, Hollywood-inspired violence. You'd think the average murderer needs inspiration as much as any artist. If he's not murdering someone at the moment, it's probably because he's got a bad case of killer's block.

Obviously it was Sara's recent story that turned my thoughts in this direction. She wrote about a beautiful, self-absorbed woman named Nika—a young woman much like herself—who was pursued by an artist in search of inspiration. That artist, Mario Migliori, whom she regarded as a charlatan if not a psychopath, was obviously supposed to be me. But who was the "muse of violence" in the story's title? Was it Nika, who was enlisted to inspire Mario in his art—and in his violence, if he was really a serial killer? Or Mario himself, who inspired Nika to perfect the art of snapping a man's neck before he could do her any harm? And what was the story trying to tell us about the violence that had decimated our group? A muse doesn't have to be a woman—Sara had insisted on that as we walked back from Brian's funeral. But in our case, if there was a muse of violence, it could only have been Jackie. Jackie was the one who'd triggered hostility in every member of the group before the violence began. Somehow she had inspired the first act of violence—her own murder—and ignited the reign of terror we were all living through. If she'd been able to turn the tables on her killer, as Sara imagined Nika doing, she could have deflected the wheel of violence before it spun out of control and crushed her. But then her own acts would have had their reverberations, as she tried to hide her complicity in the endless cycle of causes and effects. And what about me? Wasn't I (as Detective Falcone had said) the common thread that united all the victims?

Sara's Journal
July 10

Will gets weirder and weirder every day. That scene with him this afternoon left me rattled. I never expected him to show up in my apartment brandishing a butcher knife. I freaked out because it reminded me of that time with Mom, which Freddy claims never happened. Got to get a grip on myself.

One funny thing: He didn't seem surprised to see what a dump my apartment is. What does that tell you? Better get on the internet and do a little more research.

Mom is calmer now as the end nears. The priest was there tonight and I think I needed him more than she did. We prayed together and I actually found myself believing what I was saying.

I left when Dad arrived. I don't know how much longer I can stand this. I'm going to call Eleanor.

Continuation by Will Schaefer

On Monday the pace of events started accelerating toward the climax we all knew was coming. I spoke on the phone with the remaining members of the group—Eleanor, Josh and Sara—and I sensed that they had all been in touch with each other. Josh said he needed to talk to me, and I didn't even ask him why. It was a measure of the anxiety and terror that had crept up on us that we didn't really need a reason to talk to each other anymore. We were all in it together, whatever it was—there could be no mistaking that now, and being separated only made the experience worse. If there was a killer in the group, wasn't it better to have them on the other end of the phone, or sitting right in front of you?

And then that afternoon something happened that changed my whole way of looking at our situation. I realized for the first time that the killer might be someone outside the group.

And I had a pretty good idea who it was.

22

After lunch I spent an hour trying to catch up on my emails and ran off to a meeting of the Work Environment Committee, which was wrestling with the question of how to protect employees with peanut allergies who worked in our peanut butter plants. Martin had asked permission to leave a little early, which I granted without a second thought. But when I returned from my meeting I caught him in my office, supposedly watering the plants. He insisted he hadn't touched any of my files, and admittedly there was nothing in his hands but the watering can, but from that moment on I never let him out of my sight. He spent long periods of time at the photocopier and the fax machine, chatting amicably with Helen, his supposed nemesis, when I approached. Later he crouched suspiciously over his computer, clicking his mouse to keep me from seeing the screen; and when he left for the day he carried a cardboard box like the one I'd seen him filling with files in my office the week before.

The sight of that carton pushed me into action. I waited behind an empty cubicle as he stepped onto the elevator, and when the doors closed I caught the next elevator down. In the lobby I was close on his heels as he slipped past the security guard and out to the crowded sidewalk. I followed him several blocks to the steps of the New York Public Library, where he met a heavy, preening older man who looked like Oliver Hardy. Where had I seen that man before? My God, it was Eleanor's husband Howard! With a sickening

jolt I saw the connection between Martin and the writers'
group: he was insanely jealous of the group, he knew when
and where the meetings took place, and he had access to the
addresses and phone numbers of the members. Why hadn't I
thought of that before?

Martin and Howard greeted each other warmly and
chatted for a few minutes before proceeding in the direction
of Sixth Avenue. Near the corner of Sixth and 44th they
ducked into a crowded bar and left me peeking through a
window in the door. I saw Martin stash his carton under a
barstool—he clamped his foot down as if it might crawl
away—and the two of them stood jabbering at close range,
drinking toasts and laughing like old friends.

On impulse I called Sara and asked her to hurry over to
the bar, which was only about three blocks from her office.
To my surprise she sounded like her old self. She didn't
mention our last awkward meeting but agreed to come over
without asking for an explanation.

"Peek through the window," I said when she arrived.
"There's a fat guy and a skinny guy standing at the left end of
the bar."

"The fat one is Eleanor's husband."

"Do you know the other one?"

"I don't think so."

"What we're trying to find out is whether he knows you."

Without hesitation she sauntered inside and threaded her
way up to the bar while I watched through the window to see
if either of the men recognized her. Howard, of course, had
seen Sara at Kate's funeral, but there was no good reason why
Martin should have known who she was. From where I
stood I couldn't see Martin's face, but I could see
Howard's—it turned the color of a bloody mary when Sara

sidled up next to him. There were nervous introductions, nervous bursts of laughter, even some nervous kisses on the cheek. But when Sara finished her drink and slipped back outside, she reluctantly reported that my little experiment had been inconclusive. Martin, if he recognized her, had done a first-class job of pretending not to. All he seemed to be interested in talking about was the stock market.

"What's in that box?" she wanted to know when we were safely around the corner. "The box Martin was holding down with his foot."

"I'm not sure." I slipped my hand behind her elbow so we could stay together in the rush hour throng. We were headed in the direction of Sparrow on West 55th, where I was hoping we could sit down for a cool drink. "Martin's been working on a project for Finance and maybe Howard's involved in that too—he does consulting work for Zunax. But more likely this is connected with the writers' group."

"The writers' group?" Sara must have had the same sinking feeling I had when I started connecting the dots. "What does Martin know about the writers' group?"

"He knows everything."

"I hope you didn't tell him anything about me."

"No, I haven't told him—"

"Has he read my stories?"

"No. I mean not unless he stole them out of my desk drawer." I was digging myself in deeper with every word—lying, actually, and Sara knew it.

She spun around to face me and grabbed my wrist in her viselike grip. "What are you hiding?"

"Nothing, Sara. I don't know what he read. Yesterday I caught him rifling through my personal files, but I made him put them back."

We had lurched to a sudden halt in the middle of the sidewalk, blocking the pedestrians who swarmed around us like killer bees. Sara stared into my face as if she were inspecting it for signs of insanity. "What do you mean, he knows everything?"

"He sends out the meeting notices. He knows everybody's phone number, knows where people live—"

She tightened her grip on my wrist. "He could be the killer."

"I think you might be right."

"But why?"

"He's pathologically jealous about the group. A few months ago he wanted to join and I wouldn't let him."

"Why not?"

"He writes like a sick chicken pecking randomly at the computer keys. Horrible stuff like you haven't read since the third grade."

At Sparrow we wedged our way up to the bar and ordered a couple of very sour margaritas. "I wish I could say we've solved the case," I said, swiveling on my barstool to face Sara. "Anyone who writes that badly is probably guilty of a lot of other crimes."

"You think it's Martin, then?"

"He has the motive, if you think pure spite is enough of a motive."

"I think it is," she said, a little too enthusiastically.

"But don't forget: this is a man who has never done a day's work in his life. It seems to me that sheer laziness, if nothing else, would disqualify him from being a serial killer."

"Too lazy to be a murderer?"

I winced as I took a sip of my margarita. "Too lazy to be such a careful, systematic one. And I refuse to believe that the murderer could be someone who's only in my life for comic relief."

She licked the salt from the edge of her margarita and lowered her eyebrows into a frown. "I wonder about Howard, though."

"What about Howard?"

"We assumed that Eleanor killed Jackie because she thought Jackie was trying to seduce Howard. But maybe there was more to it than that."

"Such as?"

"Maybe Jackie did seduce Howard. Remember, she was totally indiscriminate about who she slept with. I mean, really, she'd go to bed with any scumbag who'd buy her a drink."

I rattled the ice in my margarita and took an uncomfortable sip. "So you think Eleanor killed Jackie in revenge?"

Sara nodded sagely. "Or Howard killed Jackie to keep Eleanor from finding out."

I faked a laugh. "A man wouldn't kill a woman just because he had an affair with her and wanted to cover it up."

"Some weirdos would do anything."

Sara was starting to sound like Detective Falcone. "Maybe it was Martin after all," I said, trying to change the subject. "He rifled through my files, sneaked out with that cardboard box—"

"Howard probably paid Martin to help him get rid of the evidence. Something that was in your office. Did you have any of Jackie's stories in your files? Or any of Eleanor's?"

"I might have."

"Or any of mine?"

"No, absolutely not. I didn't have any of yours."

"You just made that up, didn't you?"

"To tell you the truth, I don't remember what was there."

She gave me a look that made me want to squirm off my barstool and sink into the floor. "Sometimes I bring people's work to the office," I stammered, "and stash it in my desk drawer until I get a chance to read it. The other night, after I caught Martin snooping in my office, I took everything I had there and ran it through the shredder."

"You're always hiding something, aren't you?"

I finally succeeded in changing the subject to Sara's job. She was right: I was always hiding something, and the way I did it, when I was with a woman, was to keep her talking about herself. Sara had a lot of interesting things to say about her boss, her coworkers and her job duties, and some of it might even have been true; but when her cell phone rang, she discreetly fell silent and left me to pick up the tab. I feigned disappointment, though in fact I'd been wondering how to make a graceful exit. Josh and I had arranged to meet at a bar in the financial district at eight o'clock.

The place was called The Slippery Slope. It wasn't my kind of place but it was close to Josh's office and an easy subway ride from midtown. I arrived a little late and found it overflowing with Wall Street brokers and bond traders of both sexes yakking at each other through toothy grins like a troop of well-dressed baboons. Josh stood awkwardly at the edge of the crowd, holding his drink—he was drinking cream soda, no ice—in both hands like a ceremonial offering. In his black suit he seemed to be absorbed in matters of incalculable importance. When he saw me he smiled shyly and made a little gesture with his drink, as if I might have trouble picking him out in the crowd.

I had always liked Josh, and seeing him in that element made me like him even more. Though he lived in the world of finance, he was shy where others were forward, thoughtful where they were impulsive, self-conscious where they were self-assured. It was too noisy near the bar so we found a booth where we'd be able to talk. A pretty waitress appeared and I ordered a double Grey Goose martini, which I shouldn't have done. She leaned toward Josh with an ironic smile. "Another cream soda?"

For a while we sat making small talk—the usual inanities about baseball and the weather. Josh's team was the Mets and they were not doing well, which he attributed to the miserable weather. As he spoke he kept close watch on an ostentatious couple beside us whose haircuts must have cost more than our suits. If one of them happened to glance in our direction, Josh lowered his voice as if he thought they'd been sent to eavesdrop on his complaints about the Mets. Sometime after I finished my second double martini—also something I shouldn't have done—the conversation came around to the reason for our meeting. The Grey Goose had taken its toll, and my recollection of what followed may not be perfect. I know I was astonished by what Josh told me but I never doubted that it was true. There was a glint of mathematical certainty in his sad, bottomless eyes.

"I don't know if I've told you this or not," he said, "but I'm an actuary. A life actuary."

"A lifer, huh?"

"That's not what it means," he said solemnly. "It means I work with life insurance, as opposed to property and casualty or some other kind of insurance."

I knew what he meant. "You calculate life expectancies and that type of thing?"

"Exactly. I have two degrees in applied math from Brooklyn College and have passed the first six qualifying exams in actuarial science. There are only three hundred life actuaries in the world who have a higher rating than I do."

"Impressive." I took another sip of my martini and let my mind drift off to less quantitative topics. For instance, there was a really attractive Asian woman standing about four feet away talking to a nerdy-looking guy who I could have squashed with one hand.

"I just wanted you to know that what you were saying the other day—the idea that there might be some connection between Paul Gratzky and what's been happening to our group—isn't as far fetched as you might think."

That got my attention. "How so?"

"Numbers have power," Josh said. " If you know how to use numbers, you can predict and control events."

"Sure. That's what insurance is all about, isn't it?"

"I'm not talking about statistical probability." He glanced over at the flashy couple to make sure they weren't paying attention. "This goes way beyond that."

"I'm not following."

He leaned closer and dropped his voice almost to a whisper. "Last year there was a major hurricane on the Gulf Coast. Hurricane Hurlene. Do you remember it?"

"Sure."

"When the weather service said the eye of the storm would pass over Corpus Christi, Texas, I was given the task of calculating the expected loss of life. I determined that 26 people would die as a result of the storm. And do you know what happened?"

"I think I can guess."

"Two days later the eye of the storm hit Corpus Christi. Exactly 26 people died. I could tell you their names and a lot more about them if you want to know."

"I'll pass."

"Not 25, not 27 or 30 or some other number. Exactly 26, just as I predicted."

"So what? Isn't it just the law of large numbers?"

"No," he insisted. "These are small numbers, very small numbers from the standpoint of statistics. I could have predicted 24 or 25 or even 35 or 40 and still been within the range of statistical probability. But instead I came down exactly on 26 and that's how many people died."

He grimaced in self-reproach and quickly turned away. In that instant I could see that his cavernous eyes had room for all the sufferings of the world.

"So do you think you caused it?" I asked him. "You think your calculations caused these people's deaths?"

He hesitated and then answered with a question: "Have you ever read a short story called 'The Nine Billion Names of God,' by Arthur C. Clarke?"

"That's science fiction, isn't it? I don't usually read science fiction."

"I grew up on science fiction," he said, smiling tentatively. "Along with comic books and baseball cards." He took a sip of cream soda and his smile vanished. "Here's what happens in the story. Some Buddhist monks in Tibet hire an American computer company to install a giant computer in their lamasery. All the American engineers know is that the computer is being used to generate and print out every possible combination and permutation of the letters of a certain alphabet. The monks have been working on this project for hundreds of years and if they had to continue without a computer it would have taken them another 15,000 years. With the computer, they expect it to take a couple of months. Just as the project is nearing completion, the monks finally tell the Americans what it's all about. They believe that the purpose of mankind is to record the nine billion names of God, and that when this task is completed the universe will have served its purpose. The Americans find this laughable until they're about to get on their plane to fly home. Just then, as the computer finishes its work, they look up at the sky and see the stars beginning to go out."

"What do you mean, 'go out'?"

"Literally *go out*, like a light. The universe has served its purpose. It's coming to an end, thanks to the monks and their computer."

I sat for a moment pondering what Josh had just said. Was I hearing him correctly? Had the Grey Goose martinis already damaged my brain? What he was saying sounded too crazy coming from an actuary—but then maybe you'd have to be crazy to be an actuary in the first place. I motioned to the waitress to bring our check.

"Nine billion," Josh said after a while. "That's about how many times Gratzky trades every day."

Suddenly I understood why he was telling me this. "What are you saying? Gratzky's trying to bring the world to an end by computing the nine billion names of God?"

Josh shook his head. "In my religion, God has only one name and we are forbidden to say it. You're missing the point."

"What point?"

"The story isn't about God. It's about us, don't you see? It's trying to tell us that our mathematical calculations could have consequences we can't even dream of. This has always been true, but the process used to be so slow we didn't notice it. What used to take eons can now be done in a few seconds with a supercomputer."

"This is still science fiction, right?"

"No, this is for real."

The waitress brought our check and Josh insisted on paying it, even though he drank only cream soda. All I could think of was getting out of that bar, but once we were outside in the sulfurous heat I wished I was home listening to anonymous death threats. I tried to say goodbye but Josh dogged my steps to the subway like a panhandler.

"You're probably asking: What does this have to do with Gratzky and his hedge fund?" he said as we walked past City Hall.

"I'm not even asking."

"Gratzky's supercomputers seek out little gaps and variations in prices around the world, and when they find the tiniest gap, even if it only exists for a fraction of a second, they zoom in and trade on it. They do this about nine billion times a day."

"So what?"

"Don't you see? The more they trade on those little gaps, the more the gaps are narrowed. What they're doing is eliminating all the outlying values, crowding everything closer to the mean. If this goes on long enough, the bell shaped curve becomes a straight vertical line, with all the values exactly at the average. And Gratzky controls the world."

At last, to my relief, we had reached the subway station. Without a backward glance I plunged down the stairs, confident that not even an actuarial zealot would follow me into that steaming hellhole. But Josh marched down right behind me, his black suit drenched with sweat, and slipped a card into the turnstile to continue his pursuit.

"Gratzky controlling the world," I said when we reached the crowded platform. "Is that what this is all about?"

"Don't worry," he said. "It can't go on that long. It can't go on long enough for him to succeed."

"Why not?"

"Because when you push this process too far, it turns around on you. When everything has reverted to the mean, when every value has been squeezed into the average, you get an opposite reaction. Crazy random events seem to pop out on the edges. That's what I think has happened to Gratzky and his family and business associates. I call it *the revenge of the improbable*."

"But what happened to those people wasn't just blind chance."

"Of course not."

"Some of them were murdered."

"I'd be surprised if they weren't."

There was something alarming, even menacing, in the way he said that. At some point during my descent into the subway station it had dawned on me that Josh might be crazy enough to have murdered Jackie and Brian and Kate. Maybe my number was up—maybe I had to die for actuarial reasons, if nothing else. This Fourth of July Weekend, they'd said on the radio, Don't become a statistic! Is that what they meant?

The train was pulling into the station. Either of us could have pushed the other one down on the track and in all likelihood no one would have seen him do it. I tried to step backwards but the crowd was surging in behind me, pressing me closer and closer to the track and the oncoming train. I looked in Josh's eyes and what I saw there, in light of what happened later, is something I will never forget. Sadness, desperation, guilt—above all guilt

I shouldered my way backwards into the crowd, triggering some angry curses and shoves from the people behind me. Would Josh pursue me onto the train? I knew what I would do: I'd wait till the last minute and jump on right before the doors closed. "What do you mean you'd be surprised if they weren't?"

"You see," Josh said with a peculiar smile, "when something has to happen, it doesn't matter *how* it happens. If those people around Gratzky had to die, they had to die no matter what. Some were killed in accidents or died of rare diseases, a few committed suicide—and yes, there were some who were deliberately murdered. But even if they were all murdered by a dozen different murderers or by the same murderer, for a dozen different reasons or for no reason at all, and even if the murderer never heard of Gratzky and his calculations—they died for only one reason. They died because they had to die."

"How can you believe that?"

"The 26 people who died in Corpus Christi were doing all sorts of things that day." Josh raised his hands and started counting on his fingers. "Some went to work, some stayed at home. Some boarded up their windows, some tried to flee to higher ground. Maybe even some of them died of natural causes or were murdered in their beds at the height of the storm. It doesn't really matter."

The train had glided to a stop in front of us. The doors opened and the crowd pushed their way past the arriving passengers into the car. I stood my ground and darted inside just in time to duck between the closing doors. Josh was right behind me, clamping his hands between the doors and prying them apart with all his strength to keep them from closing. He stared at me through the opening and I could hardly bear the sadness in his eyes. "All those people died because they had to die on that particular day," he said, before he lost his grip. "Just as I predicted."

23

The next morning I was prepared to confront Martin but he had already called in sick. His nemesis Helen—who I was now beginning to suspect was his accomplice—smirked as she offered backup assistance, knowing full well that Martin never did any work. Even the security guard at the front desk seemed to be in on the joke. He gave me his usual sober nod, but as I walked past him I could have sworn I saw him wink. I found the morning mail heaped on my desk, my wastebasket overflowing with yesterday's trash. There was no paper in the printer, no water in the water cooler, no coffee in the coffee machine. But if there was handwriting on the wall, I didn't notice it.

My thoughts were on Sara, who had stopped returning my increasingly frantic phone calls. She'd been annoyed when I confessed that Martin might have found some of her stories in my office. Was that why she wasn't calling me back? Or was there some other explanation I didn't even want to think about? The danger seemed to be pressing in from too many directions. First Eleanor and now Howard, Martin and Josh—I couldn't keep track of so many suspects. Martin was feigning illness, Howard (as I learned from Helen) was not expected in the office, and only God or the law of averages could predict where Josh might turn up. Any one of them could have had Sara locked in their sights at that very moment. How could I protect her if she wouldn't return my calls?

Just as I began to imagine that things couldn't be any worse, the phone on my desk buzzed and I picked it up. It was Detective Falcone.

"Come out to the street," he said, "and look for a cab."

"I'll never get a cab out there."

"You'll get one," he said, and he hung up.

I hurried outside and stepped to the curb, raising my hand futilely against the surging traffic. I might as well have been King Canute ordering back the waves as trying to hail a cab on Lexington Avenue at that time of day, but miraculously a yellow cab pulled up beside me and stopped. The driver leaned over and signaled for me to climb in. It was Detective Falcone.

"Don't act like you know me," he said, pulling away from the curb. "Somebody might be watching."

"Who?"

He gave no answer, whipping the cab through the traffic to some unknown destination. We raced downtown as far as 34th Street and then wove our way across town to Penn Station, where Falcone parked at the end of a long line of cabs waiting to pick up fares at the station. "We can sit here for a while," he said. "Get in front."

I climbed out and slipped into the front seat. Falcone tipped down both visors and squinted at me with his dark, unforgiving eyes as if I was a lower form of life. He wore the same Yankees jacket he'd been wearing when we met at Starbucks. "Your week is almost up. You got anything for me?"

"What do you mean?"

"I mean, you got anything for me?"

He swiveled toward me, angry at my hesitation. "Like I told you, if you're not going to cooperate there's plenty of people who'd like to take a crack at you."

"I'm cooperating," I said. "I appreciate your efforts."

"What have you got?"

I had to give him something and there was no way it was going to be about Martin or Howard or Josh. I felt a flush of shame as I replied, as if I were denouncing my best friend to the secret police. "Last time we met I tried to tell you about a woman in the writers' group named Eleanor."

"Yeah, I know who she is."

"Good." I took a deep breath, conscious that whatever I said, this was not going to be a pleasant conversation. "Well, the night you came to my apartment she had just read a story to the group that was like an eerie premonition of Jackie's murder. The main character was a middle-aged woman a lot like Eleanor and she hated a younger woman who was a lot like Jackie. She followed the younger woman home on the subway and then went to her front door with a letter opener in her purse that—"

"What's the point of all this?" Falcone glared back at me with mocking eyes.

"Well, isn't this a lot like the real murder?"

"It was just a story, you said. We're talking real life here."

"I know, but doesn't it seem a little too close to be a coincidence?"

"If you say so." He acted like he was humoring me. "So how did the story end? Did she kill the woman?"

"Eleanor still hadn't written the ending. At least that's what she told us."

He made a puzzled face. "Why didn't you tell me about this that night?"

"We were all in a state of shock." I slipped sideways, as far away from Falcone as I could get. He pushed a button on his left and the locks on all the doors snapped shut. I didn't know if I could get out of the cab or not. Even with the air conditioner blowing at me, I could feel the sweat dripping down my forehead. "First," I said, trying to stay calm, "when Eleanor read her story we had no idea Jackie was dead. We only learned about it from you. And then when you told us the details and we saw the resemblance of what you described to Eleanor's story—I guess we just couldn't believe it."

Falcone took his time before responding. "I can see why you didn't want to say anything in front of her," he said calmly. "But why didn't you call me the next day?"

"We thought about it—I thought about it, and I decided it would be an over-reaction. There really wasn't enough evidence to accuse somebody of murder. It was"—I felt ridiculous saying this—"a privacy issue."

"A privacy issue! Who else was involved?"

"What do you mean?"

"You said 'we.' Who else was thinking about it with you?"

"Nobody. I didn't—"

"The Latina?"

"Sara? Is that who you mean?"

He snorted derisively. "The one you've been stalking. Is that who you talked about it with?"

"Yes."

"And the two of you decided not to call me." He shook his head in scornful disbelief. "Don't you realize you're covering up a murder? *Conspiring* to cover up a murder, I ought to say."

"No, we aren't," I insisted. "We didn't think Eleanor really did it. She had an alibi. She said she told it to you."

The pick-up line had advanced in front of us. Without taking his eyes off me, Falcone put the car in gear and moved it forward to fill in the gap. Then for about two minutes he sat studying me as if I were a stuffed specimen of some endangered species in the Natural History Museum. "All right," he finally said in a low voice. "Why didn't you call me when Brian Maynes was killed?"

"They said it was an accident."

"You thought it was just a coincidence that two members of your writers' group were killed within a week?"

His voice sounded sarcastic now, but I stayed calm, maybe too calm for what he was setting me up for. "We didn't know," I said. "There was no reason to believe Eleanor might have killed Brian. And frankly, we were afraid—I was afraid—that you'd do what you're doing now. That you'd blame me, or suspect me, for not calling you sooner."

"I saw you at the funeral. You didn't exactly look grief stricken."

I glared back at him coldly. "I didn't kill him, if that's what you're suggesting."

Falcone seemed amused at my show of indignation. "What about the next murder?"—his tone was even more sarcastic than before—"Did you think that was a coincidence too?"

"I'd already made up my mind to call you when you called me."

"What did your cute friend think?"

"Sara? She completely agreed."

"But you waited—for no good reason—and killed two more people. I hope that makes you feel good." He watched me carefully.

"I didn't kill anybody," I said, wiping the sweat from my forehead.

The denials were sounding lame and perfunctory even to me. "Don't I get a Miranda warning?" I asked as Falcone moved the cab forward in the line.

"You're not being questioned," he said. "And you're not in custody. You'll know when you're being questioned." He slipped the car out of gear and turned to face me so he could watch me squirm. "So why didn't you tell me when we met at Starbucks?"

"You mean about Eleanor? I tried to tell you but you didn't give me a chance. You basically told me to shut up."

"You were about to tell me and I told you to shut up? Give me a break!"

"I wanted to tell you. I tried to—"

He cut me off with a wave of the hand. "If I didn't want to hear about Eleanor, maybe it was because I already knew all about her."

"What do you mean?"

"I know all about Eleanor and her story."

"You do?"

"Sure I do. Even though you and the Latina chose to jack me around for two weeks—conspiring to hinder and delay a homicide investigation—not everybody in your little group was so stupid. In fact there were others—don't bother asking me their names—who did the right thing and called my cell phone as I requested and gave me the information you and your girlfriend deliberately withheld from my investigation."

I couldn't believe what I was hearing. "So you've known about Eleanor all along?"

"I've even read the story. It's a piece of crap, in my opinion. But I admit there's a resemblance to the actual facts. I've had a man watching her day and night. If she's been out killing people she must have wings."

"Then why did we just have this conversation?"

"You've been jacking me around for two weeks," he smirked. "Just returning the compliment."

We had reached the front of the line, where a dispatcher who served no apparent purpose pointed a row of sweltering travelers to the waiting cabs. A man in a dark suit stepped toward us and just as he reached the car Falcone sped away, leaving him shouting in frustration on the curb. We lurched ahead and joined the rest of the flotsam bobbing on Eighth Avenue, jolting to a sudden stop at the first red light.

"What's happened since you talked to me last week?" he asked.

"On Saturday we all went to Kate's funeral on Staten Island."

"All of you? Who went?"

"Eleanor, Josh, Sara and myself. And Eleanor's husband Howard."

"The fat guy? I have a man on him too."

"I'm sure you do."

"You all came back on the ferry together?"

I could tell he already knew the answer to that question. "Obviously the police were watching," I said. "I thought I noticed a taxi following me home."

The light changed and Falcone had to decide which way to go. "You want to go back to your office?"

It was almost three o'clock by now and I couldn't bear the thought of returning to work. My boss, his boss and the rest of Zunax senior management had dropped off the face of the earth and I had to get ready for the writers' group meeting that night. "You know where I live," I said. "Why don't you just take me home?"

We drove quietly down to Chelsea, like a couple of friends returning after a pleasant afternoon. Falcone stopped the cab about a block from my apartment, and before he let me go he asked a few more questions. His tone of voice was no longer sarcastic. It was quiet and thoughtful, as if he cared about the answers.

"What did you and Sara talk about on the ferry?"

"We didn't have much to say to each other. She was depressed about the funeral."

"Did you talk to Eleanor? What was she acting like?"

"Normal. As normal as could be expected."

"What about the magician?"

"Josh?"

"Yeah, Josh." Falcone broke into a broad smile. "Nice Jewish boy who dresses like a magician. You met him in a bar downtown last night. Did he do any tricks for you?"

"Nope." The last thing I wanted to discuss with the police was Josh's cosmic number theories or the possible influence of Paul Gratzky. "We talked about his work," I said blandly. "He's in the insurance business. Pretty dull stuff."

Falcone chuckled as he snapped the door locks open, motioning for me to go. "If Josh tries to sell you any life insurance," he called after me as I climbed out of the cab, "maybe you should give it some serious consideration."

* * *

At home that afternoon I checked my messages—still nothing from Sara—and tried again to reach her on her cell phone, her office phone, her home phone. "Leave a message" was the closest I came to a response. Spitefully, after I'd finished cleaning my apartment—which consisted mainly of hauling empty liquor bottles down to the dumpster—I continued my internet research on her and her family, arriving at the melancholy conclusion that Detective Falcone had been right and everything she'd ever told me about herself was a lie. She was a Latina, all right, but not from Chile. She was Puerto Rican, born and raised in New York. Her father was not a surgeon, but a furniture polisher; she had never attended any fancy schools where they wore field hockey kilts, never gone to Yale or any other Ivy League college; in all likelihood she'd never studied art history or set foot outside the United States. If she'd worked at the Abrams publishing house it was probably as a receptionist or file clerk. Yet even with all those accidents of social identity stripped away, I wanted to believe that she was still the Sara I knew and loved, that there was something about her—her inner self, as it were—that I could still believe in, something that was just as true as anything she'd represented herself to be. I had read her stories, I told myself. I knew who she was.

Correction: I *thought* I knew who she was. I never seriously considered the possibility that she might be Nika, the reluctant muse, who could break a man's neck with her bare hands.

24

That night the writers' group met in my apartment for what would prove to be our final meeting. There was no small talk now, no kidding around or even any emotion. It was all very careful and businesslike. Everyone in the lifeboat knew the food and water were running out.

We sat in our usual places, avoiding each other's eyes and any reference to the empty seats or those who once occupied them. In fact the apartment seemed as crowded as ever, thanks to Howard, who took up more than his share of real estate. That evening he'd come inside with Eleanor instead of dropping her off as he usually did. Grunting a barely audible hello, he pulled up one of the kitchen chairs and perched—if a man his size could be said to perch—behind his wife, who sat in front of him like a ventriloquist's dummy. Sara came in after Eleanor and Howard, sliding into her seat without even looking at me.

Josh arrived last—it was his turn to read—and sat alone on the loveseat he used to share with Kate. He was the only one who hadn't read since Jackie set the fatal cycle in motion. I wondered if his story would be as crazy as he was.

"Well, everyone's here," I said. "Is anyone still getting the anonymous phone calls?"

Eleanor hesitated, waiting for a nudge from her husband before she answered. "Now it's ringing four times. Isn't that right, Howard?"

Howard frowned. "That's right. Four times. Private Caller, it says."

"I've started getting weird calls too," said Sara. "On my cell phone. Of course you can't count the rings with a ring tone. The music just starts and they hang up when I try to answer."

"Josh?"

"No, no," he mumbled. "Nothing so far."

Silence. Everyone must have been thinking the same thing. If we wanted to survive we could not acknowledge that the killer might be among us. We had to pretend that it was the *Other*—some unnamed, possibly unnamable outside force like the Devil or Paul Gratzky or the revenge of the improbable.

"Are 'chance' and 'fate' the same thing?" I wondered aloud.

"No, of course not," said Eleanor. "They're completely different."

"Are they opposites?"

Eleanor swiveled toward her husband, whose face remained impassive. "I don't know," she murmured.

"If you're walking down the street," I continued, "and a brick falls on your head, is that chance?"

"Yes," said Sara. "Absolutely."

"But what if you're killed in an auto accident?"

"That's fate," said Josh.

It was time to let the 800-pound gorilla out of its cage. "What I'm wondering," I said, "is about Jackie and Brian and Kate. Two of them were murdered, and the other one probably murdered, all within a matter of weeks. How could that happen?"

"Coincidence," Howard declared, clutching Eleanor's arm. "Probably nothing but coincidence." Eleanor's head bobbed up and down in agreement.

"There are no coincidences," Josh objected. "Everything happens for a reason."

"Or for no reason," Sara said.

It was time for Josh to read his story. He pulled a handwritten manuscript from his inside suit pocket and unfolded it carefully, smoothing the pages on his lap. He sat for a few minutes frowning down at the manuscript with seeming incomprehension. Then, bowing over it as if it were a sacred text, and without looking up or in any way acknowledging his audience, he began to read a story entitled "The Judgment."

Like all of Josh's stories, it was about a thirty-year-old bachelor named Allen K. who lives with his parents in Brooklyn and earns his living selling baseball cards over the internet. One morning he awakes with the conviction that he does not exist, inspired by a conversation he had the day before with the building superintendent, Mr. Berns. Allen had gone to Mr. Berns's apartment with a request from his mother to fix a leaky faucet, and Mr. Berns had explained the philosophy of Descartes, who questioned even his own existence. Allen realizes that his own philosophy is exactly the opposite of Descartes's. The more he asks himself whether he exists, the more certain he becomes that he does not. Of course the molecules that make up his brain and body exist, even his thoughts exist as electrochemical events, but he—the unique individual known as Allen K.—is just an illusion, like the characters who appear on the screen when he plays a computer game. Evolution has decided that intelligent creatures who have the illusion of a unique personal existence have a higher survival rate than those who lack such an illusion. For some reason this makes Allen remember an experiment with white mice he conducted for biology class in high school, and the recollection makes him nauseous.

Allen is engaged to a Greek-American woman named Diana whom he met at a baseball card convention. Their relationship revolves entirely around sex and baseball cards. One afternoon, after an argument with his mother about Diana, his mother goes out shopping and he notices that the leaky faucet has cured itself. He goes downstairs to tell Mr. Berns but when he taps on the superintendent's door, it swings open and he discovers his mother on the couch in a state of disarray with the superintendent on top of her. Allen feels himself inflating into a gigantic enlargement of himself, and as the lovers scramble to cover themselves with odd scraps of clothing, he speaks in a voice that surprises him, a deep Biblical roar that seems to well up from the bowels of the earth: "I condemn you to death!"

Mr. Berns's wife stumbles through the door, a plain woman of about fifty-five who seems more embarrassed than angered at what she sees. "You also!" Allen bellows. "You stand condemned as an accomplice. I sentence you to death by drowning!"

He stamps out into the narrow alleyway where the garbage cans are stored and finds a hose, and as he fills the garbage cans with water he remembers the white mice and what he did to them. It was a clever experiment gone bad, an attempt to measure changes in the behavior of six mice if they were deprived of food. After a couple of days he went down to inspect the cage and discovered that three of the mice were missing. Then he found their gnawed-off tails and feet in the sawdust and knew what had happened. The mice that were left looked as cute and dumb as they always did, but they were monsters who had eaten their own mother. An explosion of moral outrage overcame him, such as he had never experienced before. He picked up the cage and carried it outside to where the garbage cans were lined up in the alleyway. He filled one of the garbage cans with water and dropped the cage into the water and stood watching the mice struggling at the top of the cage with their little pink feet and noses, and while they were still struggling, before he vomited into the water, he said: "I sentence you to death by drowning!"

"*That judgment*," Josh concluded, his voice quavering with the fury he'd breathed into Allen K., "*like the ones he had just handed out, was just and irrevocable. He filled three garbage cans with water and turned off the hose. Then he went back inside to find the superintendent.*"

When he stopped reading, Josh stared down at his story as if he was as shocked by the ending as everyone else. He folded the pages carefully and slid them back into his suit pocket, keeping his eyes down. The apartment echoed with stunned silence as if a bomb had gone off. No one spoke, no one breathed or shifted in their seat. No one wanted to end up like the white mice. Or like Jackie and Brian and Kate.

Eleanor and Sara seemed on the verge of tears. Howard's face had turned as white as the drowning mice. Even I, who always counseled against identifying an author with his characters, was reluctant to continue with the meeting. The character in Josh's story was so obviously himself—this was not the first story he'd read us about Allen K.—that he needed to be handled with the utmost caution. To offer the slightest criticism could be potentially suicidal.

"Well," I finally said. "Sometimes a story so completely conveys what it's trying to convey that no discussion is necessary. So unless anyone objects, I think we should adjourn until next week."

There was a murmur of agreement, without any specific voice being raised. I glanced at Josh, who gave no sign of having heard what I said.

"We all have to stick together," I went on. "If there's an emergency I need to be able to reach you. So if your email address or cell phone number has changed, please call my office and leave it on my voice mail. Don't give it to my assistant—leave it on my voice mail. And you might want to share your contact information with each other in case you can't reach me."

Howard stood up to leave, pulling Eleanor up with him, and I began to gather up the empty lemonade glasses. Sara caught my eye to see if there was anything else I wanted to say.

"One other thing," I said. "Who's reading next week?"

There was a long, uncomfortable pause as we all tried to figure out whose turn it was and came to the same unsettling conclusion.

"Next week would have been Jackie's turn," I said evenly. "And so... in Jackie's absence, that means we've come back around to Eleanor."

All eyes were on Eleanor. Curious eyes, frightened eyes, pleading eyes that said: Please write something that will put an end to this cycle of death you set in motion.

"I feel like I'm on *Survivor*," Eleanor said, braving a tiny smile.

I stared back at her with a queasy sense of déjà vu. "You said that at Kate's funeral."

"Maybe she did," Howard interjected, stepping in front of her. "What of it?"

"It's like the Agatha Christie book, isn't it?" I asked Eleanor, a little too sharply. "*And Then There Were None*. Are you the one who brought that book back and left it on my table?"

She hesitated. "I don't think so."

"Of course she didn't," Howard glared. "What are you getting at?"

The others goggled back at me in confusion. "I've been meaning to ask all of you—"

But I stopped short before I finished my sentence. I was going to ask them who returned the book, but suddenly I remembered who I'd loaned it to, and it wasn't anyone in the room.

I'd loaned the book to Jackie.

25

When I arrived at work the next morning I was surprised to find Martin bustling between his desk and the photocopier, his arms laden with files. A quick glance satisfied me that the files had nothing to do with me or the writers' group. He coughed when he saw me and covered his mouth with a handkerchief, foiling my plan to confront him with a string of irrefutable accusations ranging from malingering to premeditated murder. "Are you sure you're all right?" I asked him solicitously. "You didn't have to come in today."

"Still a little under the weather," he wheezed. "But I thought I'd better drag myself in before too much work piles up."

What was I going to say? Your work as a spy, a thief and possibly a murderer is too important to go undone, even for a few days? If I got lucky, he would soon be looking for another job.

As the morning wore on I began to wonder if the rest of the department already worked somewhere else. There was no one in the men's room, no one trying to entice a cup of espresso out of the coffee machine. No one stopped me in the hall to ask what I thought about the weather. In fact, as I discovered, most of the cubicles stood empty, most of the computer screens were blank or rolling with screen savers. Could there have been a major scheduling glitch that allowed the whole department to go on vacation at the same time?

"Where is everybody?" I asked Martin when he brought in my mail.

He sat down across from me and leaned forward with a sly smile. "Where is everybody? We already know that, don't we?"

"I assume they're all on vacation."

"'Vacation,'" he repeated, as if putting the word in quotes.

"Only I don't know how the whole department could be on vacation at the same time."

"Well, we've cut back a little, haven't we? I mean, we don't really have that many people working here anymore, do we?"

I didn't like his insinuating tone. "As far as I know, we have just as many as we always had."

"That's what it says in the press releases," he agreed, coughing slightly. "But just between you and me…"

"Just between you and me," I cut him off, "I don't know what you're talking about."

"Right." He stood up and gathered a few items from my outbox. "By the way, have you heard the latest about Gratzky? He's not in the hospital—that rumor was false. But he's gone into seclusion and his lawyer won't tell where he is. The blogs are saying he's on the verge of suicide."

"I'm not surprised."

Martin stepped toward the door and then turned back around. "The stock market is down 300 points."

"How's our stock doing?"

He smiled mischievously. "Seems to be holding up so far."

I spent most of the morning trying to reach Sara with no success. After our meeting the night before, she and I had exchanged a few awkward words before she slipped out the door with Eleanor and Howard. Obviously there were a few issues we needed to discuss. She blamed me for letting her stories and personal information fall into Martin's hands, and I might have blamed her—based on what I'd learned from Detective Falcone and my internet research—for being a complete fraud. Instead I was worried sick about her, and the inconclusive answering machine messages only fed my anxiety.

The afternoon found me glued to my computer screen. Wild rumors flew through the blogosphere and would have echoed through the cubiclesphere if anybody had been at work: Gratzky was in a coma, Gratzky was in a deep depression, Gratzky was in a mystical trance, Gratzky was already dead. The stock market fell another 300 points as the outside temperature rose over 100. I did a quick cubicle check to see how many people had returned from lunch and found one analyst reading emails, two assistant managers researching severance benefits, and three secretaries surfing the web in search of better jobs. By three o'clock Zunax stock had lost ten percent of its value on a rumor that our outside auditors had resigned. The rumor proved to be true and the stock tumbled another twenty percent before the market closed. Speculation centered on second quarter earnings, which were scheduled to be announced on Friday.

I knew I should be drafting a press release, but I hadn't heard so much as a "Please handle" from Bob Tedder since the week before. I was on my own.

Venturing to the 15th Floor, home of the Finance Department, I found a similarly devastated landscape of abandoned cubicles and idling screen savers. Poor Elizabeth Grady, her eyes bloodshot, her lips pale, sat huddled at her desk surrounded by heaps of spread sheets and take-out food boxes, pulling distractedly at her straggly hair.

"Where's the head of this department?" I asked, trying not to startle her.

"Gone," she murmured without looking up. "Gone."

"And Milton Babst?"

"Gone," she said. "Still in Nepal."

"I have to draft a press release for the quarterly earnings announcement. Do you have the sales figures?"

"Don't go there."

"The manufacturing figures?"

"There aren't any."

"Quarterly earnings?"

She looked at me for the first time and laughed. "Are you kidding?"

I gestured over the empty cubicles. "Where are the bean counters?"

"We let them go," she said. "There aren't any beans left to count."

Sara finally called just as I was about to leave for the day. She'd had a busy day at work—delightfully boring, as she put it, with no threats, kidnappings or attempts on her life. She said she was sorry for blaming me about Martin; in fact she doubted that Martin or Howard had anything to do with the murders.

"So you've narrowed it down to Josh, then?" I asked, thinking of the poor white mice in the garbage can.

"No, not at all."

"Then you still think it's Eleanor?

"No. Listen"—she hesitated—"Last night you mentioned *And Then There Were None*. Have you read that book?"

"Sure, I've read it. Ten people go to an island and they get murdered, one by one."

"And in the end, who does the murderer turn out to be?"

"Well—"

"It was one of the victims."

"What do you mean?"

"It was one of the victims. No one suspected him because he was already dead."

26

On the way home I stopped for a solitary drink—Sara having brushed off my attempt to lure her to dinner—at a sleazy bar called Araby that seemed to be full of middle-aged men picking up slightly younger women who had more than their share of teeth. I thought back to the day Kate's body was found, when Sara's first thought had been of Scheherazade, the concubine summoned up from the harem to entertain the sultan with a story before he slit her throat. Scheherazade had outsmarted the sultan by keeping him in suspense, by leaving each story hanging by a thread when the morning dawned and she was obliged to fall silent. Was that what Sara was doing with her evasions and impersonations—trying to stay alive by keeping the world in suspense? Or more precisely, by keeping me in suspense, as if she thought I might be the murderer? The blonde on the next barstool must have had the same suspicion. When I smiled at her she bolted in the direction of a paunchy salesman in a brown suit.

Arriving home in Chelsea, I stumbled through the twilight gazing up at my own apartment, wondering if it was safe to live where so many people could peer through the windows. From where I stood on the other side of the street, you could see my bust of Mozart on the windowsill, my Matisse print on the wall, my St. Louis Cardinals sweatshirt draped carelessly over the closet door.

"Spying on your own apartment?" asked a woman's voice.

It was Zelda, patrolling the neighborhood with Wolfgang and her canine colostomy bag in search of new pollution opportunities. Wolfgang looked particularly depraved that night, his eyes glazed, his tongue lolling, like one of those hounds in Renaissance tapestries straining to tear some poor unicorn to shreds. Zelda herself didn't look much better. Her orange hair was beyond spiky, it was standing on end as if she'd seen a ghost, and her piercings glistened like special effects in a low-budget science fiction movie. If I hadn't known who she was I would have taken her for one of the local drug addicts or prostitutes. No one would have suspected that she was a mathematical genius who directs the investment of more money in a day than the average country spends in a decade.

"Your friend Gratzky has been going down in flames," I observed.

"I know," she said, shaking her head. "And taking the world with him."

A little shiver ran through me as I detected an echo of Josh's wacky theories. "You mean the stock market?"

"The stock market, the bond market, the whole world economy."

"You sound concerned."

"The man has more money than God," she said, flashing her eyes at me. "He may even be God. Who wouldn't be concerned?"

The markets were crashing, everybody knew that. But I wondered if Zelda's emotional reaction to my questions had a more personal origin. "Are things really that bad?" I asked her. "Or is this just because of your relationship?"

"What relationship?"

"Well, people say that you and Gratzky—"

"Listen to me," she snapped. "I'm only going to say this once: There is not and never has been anything between me and Paul Gratzky." She sounded like she was taking the Fifth Amendment. Wolfgang stood growling beside her like a defense attorney.

"All right," I said. "I guess people are wrong."

"They usually are."

I started to walk away. "Oh, Zelda," I said, turning around. "Just one thing. The phone calls have got to stop."

"What phone calls?"

"Come on. You know what phone calls. You've been making them since before all this even started."

"Since before all what even started?"

"And now you've been adding another ring every time somebody gets killed."

"Every time? What are you talking about?"

I couldn't help but laugh. "You've been keeping score pretty well for somebody who doesn't know what's going on. One ring, two rings, three rings—and always an extra ring for the next victim."

"You've gone out of your mind." She tugged on Wolfgang's leash and tried to pull him away, but he held his ground, apparently determined to hear me out even if Zelda wouldn't.

"I'm sure Kate was keeping you informed right up to the day she died."

"I have an appointment to talk to the police about Kate tomorrow." Zelda glowered at me as if I had been responsible for her friend's death. "Now I'll have something to tell them."

"They know all about it," I said, though I wasn't sure if I'd ever mentioned the phone calls to Falcone.

Wolfgang suddenly lost interest in the conversation and started pulling Zelda away, toward the corner. She followed without a word, but after about ten steps she abruptly choked back on the leash and swung around to face me. "About those phone calls," she called out, smiling maliciously. "I can't remember—what was the name of the novel Hemingway wrote about the Spanish Civil War?"

I spent the rest of the evening troubled by dark, philosophical thoughts, tinted even darker by the inordinate quantities of Irish whisky I consumed. By ten o'clock my head felt as if it had been stuffed with buckshot and detonated. I popped some popcorn and turned on the TV just in time to catch my favorite cop show. A team of typical police detectives— skeptical young men in Armani suits and brainy blondes displaying generous amounts of cleavage—were on the trail of a serial killer who had a penchant for teenage girls. They spent the hour gathering sophisticated scientific evidence, but in the end the killer (who turned out to be an executive at a large pharmaceutical firm) was caught by the simple expedient of asking him accusatory questions until he broke down and confessed. On TV the murders of Jackie, Brian and Kate would have rated a nonstop investigation involving at least fifty FBI agents checking dozens of untrustworthy suspects. We had only Detective Falcone working undercover and whatever small forces the NYPD had placed at his disposal. For reasons of economy if nothing else, they had assumed that the killer came from within the ranks of the writers' group. As far as I knew, no pharmaceutical executives had even been questioned.

I tried to imagine myself as a detective sent in to unravel the murders, like Detective Falcone or—better yet—one of those serial killer experts like Clarice Starling who profile the criminal by deconstructing his crimes. The first thing I would observe about the writers' group is that any member who could be guilty of these murders must have a Jekyll-and-Hyde personality. All of us live outwardly blameless, even laudable lives. We have friends, careers, families; we each contribute to society in our own way. For any of us to commit such crimes would require a sinister hidden self, a Mr. Hyde embodying some monstrous psychological or ideological deformity. I tried picturing Eleanor in this light—soft spoken Eleanor, who couldn't even bring herself to criticize the others' stories—and it brought a smile to my lips. And what about her buffoon of a husband? Oliver Hardy as Raskolnikov—the idea made me laugh! But if you eliminated them from suspicion for that reason you would be making a mistake. Doesn't everyone have a Mr. Hyde, a secret sharer who can be roused under certain conditions to do the things we aren't allowed to do for ourselves? At first we imagine that we can control this Mr. Hyde, summon him at will, make him do our bidding, though we may call him "evil" and righteously turn our conscience against him. But in the end we must acknowledge him as our master, like the selfish gene that rules us through its singular devotion to survival and instinctual gratification. And judging from the TV show I was watching, there was no need to look for a motive. Revenge, jealousy, hatred, greed—all the time-honored reasons for people to kill each other—have been discarded in favor of a motiveless malignancy that requires no explanation. In a strangely forgiving way we accept the murderer for what he is, a stage villain needing only to be identified, not explained. I wondered if that was what Sara meant by the muse of violence. Maybe the muse of violence wasn't a person, or a relationship between two people, but something altogether different—an instinctual motive force we prefer to think of as coming from outside ourselves, like some mythological inspiration, when in fact it's planted deep inside and only emerges in order to control us. When it inspires art we call it a muse; when it drives us to violence we deny it, or disown it, or dress it up in a fancy wardrobe of rationalizations.

A little after midnight the phone started ringing, as I knew it would after I talked to Zelda. The first ring was almost innocent, the second more alarming and insinuating. The third ring sounded defiant, almost taunting—that one was for Kate.

And the fourth ring—the one that pointed to the next victim? Yes, for the first time, there was a fourth ring. It was harsh, hateful, menacing.

The ringing stopped, though it lingered in my ears with a maddening insistence. Into my mind flashed the question Zelda had asked when I finished grilling her about the phone calls: "What was the novel Hemingway wrote about the Spanish Civil War?"

I ran into the living room and grabbed my copy of *For Whom The Bell Tolls*, wondering how it could be relevant to the subject at hand. And there was the answer, right on the title page—two lines quoted from a poem by John Donne:

"*Ask not for whom the bell tolls*," the quotation read. "*It tolls for thee.*"

* * *

Early the next morning, before my alarm went off, the phone began to ring again. I sat up in bed and listened. The phone rang four times, as it had the night before, and then it rang again. Five rings. What did that mean? Could there be another victim so soon?

I tried calling Sara but there was no answer. I ran down the hall and pounded on Zelda's door but no response came, not even a growl from Wolfgang. I ran back to my apartment and lay on my bed in a cold sweat waiting for the dawn. Over and over again I counted the group members in my pounding head—there had been seven, and Jackie, Brian and Kate were already dead. That left four: Eleanor, Sara, Josh, and myself. Five rings meant that only two of us would survive the coming day. On the radio they were predicting thunderstorms and a possible end to the heat wave.

At eight o'clock I rushed to the office, which now seemed all but abandoned. The internet was buzzing with news of a worldwide financial panic. The price of just about everything had dropped overnight in reaction to the latest rumors about Gratzky and his Hermetica Fund. It seemed that no one knew what investments the Hermetica Fund held or what they were worth—or what anything was worth, for that matter. Every asset in the world was suddenly less valuable than it had been the day before. The Secretary of the Treasury denied that a universal bailout was in the works.

I googled Sara's name and her known aliases and turned up nothing. The same for Josh. Then I searched for Eleanor and found what I was looking for. Late Wednesday evening she had fallen off the Staten Island Ferry and drowned, an apparent suicide.

It took me a minute to get my head around what I'd just read. Eleanor, the gentle lady from the Upper East Side who'd struggled to imagine enough conflict to tell a story, had drowned like a rat in the roiling waters of Upper New York Bay. Had she fallen, jumped or been pushed? And what was she doing on that barge to Hell anyway? I knew she wasn't quite what she purported to be. She was an alcoholic—I'd seen that for myself—and maybe she abused her immigrant servants or even her daughter. But was she a murderer? I felt guilty, the way you always feel when you've said unkind things about someone who dies, even if you know those things are probably true. Just because she's dead, I told myself, that doesn't mean she's innocent. In fact if she killed herself it was probably out of remorse for all the murders she committed, in which case our nightmare was over. Or was it? Just three of us were left now: myself, Sara and Josh. And Josh—how could I have forgotten?—was stark raving mad. Had Eleanor drowned like a rat—or a white mouse?

I shut down my computer and jumped in a cab to Brooklyn.

27

I'll never forget the scene in front of Josh's apartment building. Police cars with flashers on, sirens wailing, women screaming, men shouting, police radios blaring through the sweltering, humid air. Cops surrounding the building, roping off the block with yellow tape, pushing neighbors across the street. An ambulance with its lights flashing, a squad of EMTs, a gurney in the street. Near it on the sidewalk lay something that looked like it had once been a man. "Josh," I heard one of the neighbors say. "He fell off the roof."

Josh's mother had thrown herself on top of the body, screaming hysterically. A man I assumed was his father tried to pull her off but she pushed back at him, slapped at him, yelled at him as if he were the cause of her misfortune. A pair of EMTs tried to assist the father and she gave them the same treatment, holding them at bay with a spatula she must have had in her hand when she came downstairs. The men could have easily overpowered her and dragged her inside, or forced her into the ambulance to be given a sedative. But of all claims of right she had the most ancient—that of a grieving mother—and no one dared to challenge her.

"Come and get me!" she yelled at the police, waving the spatula. "Take me up on the roof and push me off like they did my son! My life is over!" She made a break for the door, presumably on her way to the roof, but two burly cops blocked her way with their arms crossed. Her husband approached again with his hands out but she swiped at him with the spatula. He stepped back, leaving her alone on the stoop to address the crowd in a stentorian voice. "My son," she lamented, "my son Joshua, who lies broken on the sidewalk, has two degrees in actuarial science from Brooklyn College. Who dares to tell me, his mother, that I can't stay here to see that justice is done? He passed three of the six examinations to be an actuary. Does anyone know how many people in the world have passed those examinations? A few hundred, most of them in places like India and Japan. God only knows how many actuaries there are at that level in Brooklyn. He was a good boy, in spite of what his father thought—Is it carved on stone tablets somewhere that everybody in this family must go into the floor covering business?—and in spite of his obsession with science fiction and baseball cards. He was engaged to be married to a very nice girl—she's Orthodox, that's all I'm going to say about her—and had a good job at a life insurance company. They're already saying he fell off the roof, or even—God forbid!—that he jumped. But what are the odds, I'd like to know, what are the odds of any such thing? What are the odds that a boy with his talents, his education, his generosity and greatness of heart—did I mention that he was also a Boy Scout leader for the black kids in Bedford Stuyvesant?—would just fall off a roof for no apparent reason? Why should a boy like that even go up on a roof? He's lived in this building all his life and he's never, ever gone up on that roof! You can ask Mr. Berns, the super. He would know if Joshua ever went on that roof. Why should he go up there? Did he keep pigeons or something? No, I saw what happened. He was sitting in the kitchen and his cell phone rang, or vibrated or whatever it does—I have to admit I don't know whether it rang or not, but I know that he suddenly reached in his pocket and pulled out his phone and a few minutes later he went out the door without a word. Without even putting his shoes on, for God's sake! My son wore a size twelve shoe. A pair of his shoes took up half the living room, so can you believe he would forget to put them on? To go up on the roof? Somebody lured him up there, somebody who called him on that phone, and he was so scared he forgot to put on his shoes. Look, there's his cell phone smashed to pieces on the sidewalk near where he fell! They pushed him off and now he lies dead in the street without his shoes on and all the police can do is stand around and talk to each other on their walkie-talkies!"

She glared across the heads of the police and the EMTs to the neighbors standing around me on the other side of the street. No one dared to answer, but there was some muttering in the crowd and the police held us back. Then Josh's father stepped up on the stoop and made another attempt to restrain his wife. He was a tall, ungainly man with a bald head and sagging jowls. When his wife pushed him away for the second time he turned to the crowd for support. "My son is dead," he declared. "That much is certain. And a mother who has lost her son deserves respect." He glanced at his wife, hoping to have earned some credit with this concession. "But so does a father, and some of the things my wife said should not go unanswered. It's true that Joshua was a good boy who did well in school. He graduated from Brooklyn College and I was proud of him. But why did he even need those degrees and all those examinations? He could have come into the floor covering business with me, especially after his brother Jonathan moved down to Maryland. He could have done that even after he got his degree. I made it very clear that the offer was still open. And another thing: he didn't wear a size twelve shoe. He wore an eleven, sometimes an eleven and a half, but never a twelve."

The crowd was losing interest and starting to drift away. I stood immobilized in a state of shock. I had thought of Josh as a fabulist, a weaver of surrealistic tales, Kafkaesque fantasies about a bizarre family that couldn't possibly exist in the real world. But here were his parents, arguing on the front stoop about his shoe size as a pool of blood formed around him on the sidewalk. Every detail, down to the name of the building superintendent, corresponded exactly to the world he described in his stories. What I had taken for fantasy was autobiography. And now his short, surreal life had come to an end. His mother thought she knew what happened but of course she didn't know about Eleanor and the others. She really had no idea whether her son jumped or was pushed.

Another shock lay in wait for me. I turned half way around and found Sara, about ten feet away, inspecting me with a cold eye. Her expression warned me not to come any closer.

"So it's down to the two of us," she said.

"I guess you could put it that way."

"Eleanor's dead and so is Josh. Who does that leave?"

"Just us," I said.

"We tried to make ourselves believe it wasn't someone in the group. We talked about statistical probabilities and civil liberties and why we shouldn't tell the police but we were just making up fairy tales, weren't we? Pretending to ourselves that we believed something we didn't really believe."

"What are you talking about?"

"It had to be someone in the group. How else would all those people have died they way they did?"

Without taking her eyes off me, she started walking, almost sidestepping, away from me and away from the crowd and the police cars and the angry lamentations. I followed her and we tangoed, never less than six feet apart, down the block of shabby apartments and bodegas and laundromats, keeping our eyes locked on each other although they never met. She turned a corner and we stared down into a grim, half-abandoned industrial zone, with no one in sight but a couple of homeless people picking through trash on the sidewalk. The sky darkened as thunder clouds bellowed warnings over the rooftops.

Sweat glistened on Sara's forehead and ran down the back of my neck. I felt in my pocket for the knife I hadn't needed for dealing with Josh.

"So you think it was Josh, then?" I said, shambling after her. "You think he killed Eleanor and then killed himself?"

"No, I don't think that's what happened at all. You heard his mother. Someone lured him onto that roof. Someone lured him up there and pushed him off."

"Who?"

"As I said, it's down to the two of us." She stopped and turned to challenge me with a twist of sarcasm in her voice. "And I know it wasn't me."

28

I took a step closer but her eyes pushed me back. And it wasn't just her eyes that made me hesitate. She held her hands raised slightly, fingers apart, as if she was doing a stretching exercise. I reminded myself that she could probably break my neck with her bare hands.

"You think it was me?" I gasped.

"This morning I had the feeling that someone was following me and now I know who it was. Did you come out here in a cab?"

"You really think I'm the killer?"

"Why not? You're a fraud. Why not a murderer?" She dodged around a pile of broken glass and continued down the sidewalk.

"Now wait a minute—"

"I've been doing some research on the internet. That story you read to the group a couple weeks ago. It was written by Cormac McCarthy, wasn't it?"

I felt short of breath, almost dizzy. "So it was," I admitted. "You caught me red handed. But that—"

"And there was another one a while back. I thought it rang a bell and I looked it up. It was early Raymond Carver."

I stumbled and tried to steady myself. "Another point scored."

"You're not even a writer, are you?"

"Not in that sense."

"Not in what sense?"

"In the sense that I actually write any more."

Sara brought my stumbling to a halt with a scorching glare. We were in front of an abandoned factory and the sidewalk was littered with scrap metal and plastic bottles and disintegrating cardboard boxes. The factory blocked the end of a dead end street, surrounded on either side by a wasteland of rubble and broken brick buildings. Two homeless people—one of them seemed vaguely familiar underneath his floppy hat and baggy clothing, and the other seemed to be a woman—stopped picking through the trash and turned to watch with dull curiosity.

"I was writing steadily until about three years ago," I tried to explain. "And then... I don't know what happened. I haven't been able to write anything for two or three years."

"Then why did you start the group?"

"I still consider myself part of the writing community. I find writers and bring them together, I work with them, help them find their voice—"

"And then you kill them."

I stared into her unflinching eyes, searching for the usual irony. It had vanished without a trace, leaving—what was it? Fear? Hatred? Madness? She was still stretching her fingers back and forth like a tigress exercising its claws.

"I didn't kill anybody," I said. "And you know it."

"How would I know it?"

"Because if it had to be someone in the group that killed all those people, and it wasn't me—which I know it wasn't— then it must have been you."

She shook her head in a pantomime of disappointment. "You're even crazier than I thought you were."

"Am I now? Am I the one who writes stories about being a serial killer? Am I the nihilist who doesn't believe in anything, the cold-blooded minimalist who hates her own mother, the post-post-modernist who's so pathologically detached from the people she's writing about—"

"Stop it!"

She lunged forward and I jumped back, reaching into my pocket to pull out the knife. When she saw the knife we both took a step backward and stood staring at each other in speechless amazement. Who would have thought this was where our relationship would take us? Who would have thought we'd end up circling each other like hungry wolves on a deserted street in Brooklyn?

The two derelicts didn't wait for an explanation. They threw their trash pickings down and dodged around a corner and out of sight while I brandished my knife at Sara and she brandished her lethal hands at me. As long as I held the knife she wouldn't try to jump me—I could do too much damage even if she succeeded in breaking my neck. And as long as she could clamp her grip around my throat there was no danger that I would attempt a first strike. I hated what I was doing. I hated threatening Sara, I hated being threatened by her. I even hated what I'd said about her writing. Her stories weren't all like that—they weren't all nihilistic and hateful and inhuman, only the most recent one. The Sara I knew from her earlier stories was a proud but caring woman, enigmatic but genuine, capable of a great love. Or was that just a wish fulfillment on my part, a preconceived notion unrelated to reality? With all my strength I resisted the conclusion that she was the killer. But who else? I asked myself. Who else could it be?

Then something almost inexplicable happened. Instead of keeping my eyes on Sara, as I knew I should, I found myself looking over her shoulder at a sign on the abandoned factory behind her. 'PRIVATE PROPERTY,' the sign said. 'ZUNAX CORPORATION.' Evidently the building we stood in front of belonged to Zunax, but I knew that was impossible. Zunax had a factory in Brooklyn but obviously this wasn't it. This place was all boarded up and even the graffiti looked old. Our Brooklyn factory had over two thousand employees and generated revenues of over ten million dollars a quarter. Under the sign I could see a security guard emerging through a gap in the chain link fence.

"Hey!" I shouted. "Where is everybody?"

"Ain't nobody here but us chickens!" the man said, scooting out of sight. He wore a tattered blue jacket but he wasn't a security guard. He was just another homeless schizophrenic.

Sara could have pounced on me while my attention was diverted but she didn't move.

"Speaking of frauds," I said, a little unsteady on my feet, "I've done some investigating of my own. You're not from Chile and your father isn't a surgeon in New Jersey. You grew up in Queens. Your mother lives in a shabby nursing home on Queens Boulevard."

"I'm Puerto Rican," she said icily. "My father is a furniture refinisher. My mother is dying of cancer, if that's all right with you."

"And your Ivy League education?"

"Hunter College at night. That's where I learned to write. And you know what? I actually write my stories. I don't copy them from someone else."

"Sara—"

She raised her hands. "Don't take one step closer!"

My mind had been racing since I saw the Zunax sign. I felt as though I were trapped in an enormous jigsaw puzzle without knowing what it was supposed to look like in the end. Was I working on a Botticelli angel or some nightmare vision of Hieronymus Bosch? And how, if at all, did Zunax fit into the picture? I'd never been more confused in my life but at the same time I felt close to solving the puzzle. I was desperate—I realize now—to prove to myself that Sara wasn't the killer. A flashback of the derelict in the floppy hat raced through my mind and I realized who he reminded me of—it was Martin! There was something both devious and dull in the way he slouched and turned away, something resentful in his eyes when he momentarily raised them before slipping around the corner, that triggered an image of Martin skulking around the photocopier when he was supposed to be doing something else. Did I think of that just because I was standing in front of an abandoned Zunax building that wasn't supposed to exist? Hadn't Martin asked me about this factory just a couple of days before?

"Sara," I said. "I know who the killer is. It isn't either of us."

"You're half right," she said, keeping her ironic distance.

"It's Martin. Don't look now but I think he's one of the derelicts hiding in that building behind you."

She shot a glance over her shoulder at the abandoned factory, where the man I'd mistaken for a security guard was banging his fist on one of the boarded windows. "You must think I'm an idiot," she said.

"We've got to trust each other or we won't get out of here alive."

There was more noise and I caught a glimpse of one of the derelicts peering at us from inside the factory. The one who reminded me of Martin was nowhere in sight, but the other one, the one I thought might be a woman, lurched out of an opening in the wall and walked toward us.

Sara and I faced each other desperately, both unwilling to make the first move. I didn't know whether to hate her or love her, to rescue her or run away from her. The tension was almost unbearable.

A yellow cab swung around the corner and screeched to a halt beside us. I was frightened at first and so was Sara, but then we realized it was Detective Falcone. "You're both in danger here," he said, leaning his head out the car window. His expression was grim. "Get in and I'll explain."

Sara opened the back door opposite the driver and slipped into the cab as if she'd hailed it on Fifth Avenue. I climbed warily into the back seat on the opposite side. Although I'd slid the knife back in my pocket, I kept my hand on it in case Sara gave me any trouble. I sensed—and wanted to believe—that fear and shared relief would overcome our mutual distrust. It smelled like stale cigarette smoke in the cab.

"Josh is dead," I told Detective Falcone through the plexiglass barrier that separated us.

"I know," he said. "That's why I'm here."

"How did you find us?" Sara asked.

He pushed some buttons to lock the doors and windows so he could turn up the air conditioner. "I've been keeping track."

"It's Martin, isn't it?" I asked. "I saw him back there in that abandoned factory."

The blower drowned out his response. "Where are we going?" I yelled into the little hatch in the plexiglass barrier.

"Relax!" he shouted, closing the hatch. "We'll be there in a minute."

"I guess we're going to the police station," I said to Sara, trying not to show my alarm.

She watched me apprehensively. "They've got you," she muttered, flashing a warning not to move any closer. "It's not Martin. It's you. He's taking you in."

It was the cab ride from Hell—or to Hell, as it seemed. Falcone drove through the ramshackle streets at breakneck speed but we never seemed to arrive at the police station. After ten minutes we were swerving around abandoned cars and piles of trash in near darkness beneath an elevated highway. We must have been somewhere near the ocean—I caught a glimpse of marsh grass beyond the viaduct—but apart from that I had no idea where we were. If this was still Brooklyn we must have reached the last exit, a depopulated urban wilderness not shown on any map. When Falcone slammed on the brakes and the car skidded to a halt, we could hear traffic pounding over our heads on the viaduct like the drumbeats of some savage ceremony.

Falcone jumped out, threw my door open and snapped handcuffs on my wrists before I knew what was happening. Then he yanked me out like a piece of cheap luggage and dropped me face down on the pavement.

"What are you doing?" I yelled, struggling to get back on my feet.

"I've been saving the two of you for last."

"The two of us?" I glanced in at Sara but Falcone pushed me back down.

"Give me your cell phone!" he shouted at Sara, brandishing a knife. She tossed it out and Falcone kicked it into a storm sewer. "Stay in the car!" He stood over me with the knife.

"Who are you?" I demanded.

"Don't think I'm going to fall for that! You know who I am."

"I thought you were a cop."

One of his feet was pressing down on my back "You're not too smart, are you, writer boy? Don't know much about the real world, do you?"

"Mr. Falcone—"

"You think you can sleep with my wife and get away with it?"

"Your wife? Who the hell is your wife?"

"And you can have her write it up with all the details for everybody in your little psycho group to listen to and laugh about over and over again?"

"What are you talking about?"

He leaned his weight down, trying to roll me over on my back. I resisted, curling my legs up under my chest. With my hands cuffed in front of me, I could defend myself—maybe even get hold of my knife—if I could somehow get back on my feet. If he turned me on my back I'd be at his mercy.

"I'm talking about her having sex with you," he said, kicking me in the ribs, "and every other guy she met at work or picked up at the airport and then writing about it to entertain you and your kinky circle of friends. That's what I'm talking about."

He kicked me again. Instinctively, I brought my knees up farther and curled my arms over my head.

"Jackie?" I yelled. "Are you talking about Jackie?"

"That's right. Jackie was my wife."

I raised my eyes to get a better look at him. "You're Larry?" I couldn't believe it. "Larry's a wimp, a balding guy with glasses who's the coach of the chess club—"

"I'm not Larry, you jackass!" He kicked me in the face and clamped his foot down on my throat. "Do I look like Larry? Larry was Jackie's father. She never had the balls to put me in her stories. I was her husband."

"You're the one who killed everybody. You even killed Jackie. I can't believe it!"

"You better believe it because you're next."

"But why? Why are you doing this?"

He glanced over his shoulder at Sara, huddled sobbing in the back of the cab. "It was exciting to hear all those sex stories, wasn't it?" he taunted her. "Made you feel superior? Gave you a few laughs? Well, the two of you aren't going to be laughing at me any more. No, you and the others—they're already dead—pretty soon you'll be history."

I glanced around desperately, hoping to find something I could use as a weapon. There was a pile of junk on the sidewalk about thirty feet away—construction debris, or more likely demolition debris: bricks, lumber, metal pipes. If I could get over there I might have a fighting chance even with my hands cuffed together.

Falcone lowered his voice: "In a few minutes everybody who ever read those stories will be dead."

My heart pounded with terror. "But why?"

"That's the way it has to be," he sighed, as if momentarily pacified by the prospect of completing his grisly work. "There was stuff in those stories that nobody was allowed to know."

With a painful squirm I freed my throat and slammed my cuffed hands behind his knee, throwing off his balance just long enough to roll under him and bring him down on top of me. I don't know where I got the strength to knock him over and roll toward the pile of junk on the sidewalk. I grabbed a piece of metal tubing and threw it at him as he scrambled after me. That slowed him down about half a second, just long enough so I could raise myself half way up before he yanked me back down to the pavement. I found a brick in my hand and slammed it into his shoulder, buying another half second to roll away and lurch to my feet. He picked up a wooden plank studded with rusty nails and came after me flailing it like a berserker. I dodged behind a light pole and held him at bay with an old dresser drawer while I caught my breath and searched for an escape route. On the other side of the viaduct, a weathered access road led into the marsh grass.

"Go ahead, run away!" Falcone laughed. "Your girl friend and I need to spend a little quality time together!" He jammed his plank inside the door of the cab so Sara couldn't pull it closed. I could see her huddled in the corner of the back seat.

"I'll get him, Sara!" I shouted, though I doubted if she could hear me over the pounding of the trucks on the viaduct. Anyway it was a false promise—with my hands in handcuffs I wouldn't be able to fend off the insane Falcone much longer. "I won't leave you here!"

He picked up a jagged two-by-four and stood swinging it around like a batter in the on-deck circle. He knew I had no chance of beating him if he caught up with me. What could I do? I couldn't leave Sara there by herself, but then neither could he. Was there someplace within a block or two I could run to for help?

Suddenly he was on me, whaling after me with the two-by-four. He knocked me down before I could jump out of the way. Then he pinned me down with his foot, jamming it into my throat while he leaned the board into my stomach. If I tried to move he kicked me with his other foot. In ten seconds I was going to be strangled or have my throat cut with a jagged two-by-four.

Then salvation arrived in the form of a black Mercedes sedan with tinted windows and Connecticut plates. It stopped about ten steps from where Falcone was torturing me. The driver rolled his window down and stuck his head outside. He looked like an investment banker who'd taken a wrong turn off the expressway. "Is everything all right here?" he asked Falcone.

I couldn't make an intelligible sound. "Yeah, everything's OK now," Falcone said. "This scumbag tried to hold up my cab but I got the jump on him and called the police. They'll be here in a couple minutes."

"You sure you're OK?"

Falcone nodded. "Yeah, I'm OK. Thank you, sir. No need to wait around."

As the Mercedes glided away, I pushed against Falcone with all my strength and kicked his feet out from under him. Leaping up, I ran toward the car and it slowed down, almost came to a stop. But just I came alongside the driver's window, it took off like a rocket, leaving me frozen in despair. Falcone was on top of me in a flash, slamming me into the pavement. With two savage kicks he turned me on my back. I tried to roll away but he stomped down hard on my face and bent over with his knife an inch in front of my eyes.

"That's enough fooling around," he said with an odd, weary smile. His eyes told me I wasn't going to get another chance. He'd enjoyed our little cat and mouse game and now it was over. He could kill me in peace.

Falcone's moment of peace lasted only a moment before it was overtaken by a denouement that was almost as violent and frightening as the one he intended. I saw Sara's hands around his jaw, I saw his neck whip to one side and back again, I felt him collapsing on top of me, slicing my cheek an inch from my right eye as the knife came down. I pushed him off and rolled away, gasping for breath, and lay on the pavement trying to cover my face with my handcuffed wrists as I broke down and bellowed in a mixture of crying and laughter. Sara stood over Falcone staring down at her hands.

After a moment she knelt to check his pulse. Finding him alive, she fished in his pocket for the key to the handcuffs and used it to unlock my wrists. Then she snapped the handcuffs on Falcone with his arms behind his back.

"Are you OK?" she asked me.

"Yeah, I'm fine." I had pulled myself up into a sitting position. "Except for this." I pointed to my cheek, which had already dripped a surprising amount of blood over my shirt.

"It'll be all right." She took a handkerchief from her purse and folded it into a bandage. "Here, hold this on it."

We opened the trunk with Falcone's keys and found a belt, which we used to tie him up more thoroughly. Then we lugged his unconscious body onto the back seat and locked him in.

"What about him?"

"He'll probably be all right, too."

We stood quietly for a few minutes catching our breath and trying to think about what to do next. It was starting to rain as the thunder clouds finally began their assault. Sara searched for her cell phone but it had disappeared down the storm drain where Falcone kicked it. In spite of the traffic pounding fifty feet over our heads we felt as abandoned and alone as if we'd been stranded on a distant planet.

"Well," I said, peering over the desolate landscape for some sign of civilization, "I guess we both said some things we shouldn't have said. It's understandable, though, under the circumstances, especially—"

"Stop it!"

I turned around slowly. Sara's voice sounded strained and harsh, but she was smiling at me for the first time that day. She stepped closer and I'll admit that I felt a wee bit nervous as she reached her arms around my waist. But that sensation lasted only a second or two before I wrapped mine over her shoulders and pulled her closer.

We collapsed in each other's arms and hugged each other and cried until we couldn't cry any more.

29

There's no precise word for the emotion a man feels gazing into the eyes of a woman who has just saved his life by breaking another man's neck with her bare hands. Astonishment, awe, gratitude, embarrassment, horror—as I stood there hugging Sara I felt all of those and more, clamoring together in an exhilarating sensation that might have been love. Sara seemed bedazzled, like a fairytale princess who has just discovered her own magical powers. With an air of unreality we glided into the cab and drove through the driving rain to the nearest hospital, where the EMTs quickly sized up the situation—Falcone unconscious and hog-tied on the back seat—and called the police.

After the wound in my cheek had been attended to, Sara and I sat in the waiting room across from a TV that was tuned to Fox News. "Sara," I said, "I apologize for deceiving you about my writing. I know it was wrong."

She stared straight ahead as if entranced by the TV. "What about the rest of your story—the lumberjacking in Oregon, the fishing in Alaska, the travels in South America—was there any truth in that?"

"Most of that was true," I said after a pause. "Or at least"—I couldn't help smiling—"based on a true story."

"Who am I to complain?" she shrugged. "My whole life is fake."

I squeezed her hand, which was surprisingly cold. "I won't ask about your past if you don't ask about mine."

She leaned forward and buried her face in her hands. "What I did to that man…." Her voice trailed off.

"The neck thing?"

"It's illegal to do that move from behind."

"But it was self defense. I'm sure that when you tell the police—"

"I can't tell them anything," she cut me off. "I have a record."

"Oh." I assumed she wasn't talking about Frank Sinatra or the Beach Boys. "In that case"—I groped for words— "you probably… shouldn't say anything."

For several minutes she followed my advice, sobbing noiselessly. "I don't care about your past," I said. "I've read your stories. I know who you are."

If Sara responded I can't remember what she said. My attention was captured by a news story unfolding on the TV screen. Disaster had finally struck Wall Street as a tidal wave of selling engulfed the market, knocking the blue chips down three thousand points and shattering smaller stocks in its wake. The immediate trigger was an announcement confirming that Paul Gratzky had been institutionalized and the Hermetica Fund was in the process of liquidation. As banks and institutional investors scrambled to unwind their positions, the biggest loser had been Zunax Corporation, whose stock plunged ninety-seven percent in two hours on a report that all its capital was tied up in the Hermetica Fund. Live camera crews reported from in front of Zunax Headquarters—my office!—where a jeering mob of investors and pensioners threw rocks at Zunax employees as they left for lunch.

I was so engrossed in what I saw on the TV that I hardly noticed the cop standing in front of me, smirking as he sized me up. "You did quite a job on that guy's neck," he said, as if paying me a compliment.

"It was self-defense." I pointed to my bandaged cheek. "He had a knife and was trying to kill me with it. So I just grabbed hold of his head and twisted sideways. Like you see in the movies."

"He's going to be paralyzed for life."

"The guy's a murderer. He killed his wife and four other people."

The cop's face went slack. "You have the right to remain silent," he said tonelessly. "Anything you say can and will be held against you."

"Am I under arrest?"

"Not yet."

The smirk crept back over his face as he turned and walked out of the waiting room.

Sara and I were allowed to leave the hospital about an hour later. The police took copies of our drivers' licenses and told us not to leave the city. The nurse advised me to see a doctor in five days to have my stitches removed.

"You didn't have to take the rap for me," Sara said when we were safely outside.

"I know," I said. "But I did it anyway. Go figure."

I wish I could report that I felt heroic. My back ached, my arms and shoulders were bruised, my face was painful and swollen. Spiritually I was still down on that pavement with my hands locked in front of me, getting ready to plead for my life. I would have felt much better if I'd been able to puff myself up a little, take credit where credit was due, put on a Sidney Carton act even if it made me seem vain and pompous. But I just didn't have it in me, not that day, not any day. I never claimed to be the hero of this story. I'm only the narrator.

At the corner of 39th and Lexington news reporters and politicians stood in the rain denouncing Zunax Corporation for the TV cameras against a backdrop reminiscent of the French Revolution. An angry mob had encircled Zunax headquarters, chanting threats and slogans, and if a guillotine had been set up in Times Square there would probably have been a steady stream of tumbrels carrying accountants and secretaries to their doom. The company's senior management—what was left of them—had absconded via the rooftop helicopter pad at the first sign of trouble, leaving their underlings to contend with the mob. Foolishly, I flashed my badge and was admitted to the lobby, where an FBI agent named Gordon R. Quimby backed me into a corner and proceeded to take my deposition.

"Did you draft this press release about the quarterly earnings report?" he demanded, waving a sheaf of papers. "Were you aware that the Brooklyn plant has been closed for three years?"

"I got all my information from Finance," I answered, my mind reeling.

"How much was spent on the healthcare assistance program for child laborers in Southeast Asia?"

"Why don't you ask Bob Tedder?" I cried. "He's the head of this department!"

Agent Quimby looked grave. "I understand that Mr. Tedder resigned last week to spend more time with his family. In any case we've reviewed his emails and found that he did nothing wrong." His eyes narrowed with prosecutorial zeal. "You're the one who seems to have been responsible for 'handling' things around here."

"But—"

"Don't even think about denying it. We already have copies of all your documents."

"How did you do that so quickly?"

"Oh, your assistant, Martin—what's his last name? He's been providing invaluable assistance to our investigation for over a year. Forwarding your emails, photocopying your files." Agent Quimby shook his head in mock sympathy, smirking maliciously. "Would you believe he's even been wearing a wire?"

30

Over the next few days I was able to fill in some of the blanks in the Zunax story by reading the newspapers and talking to friends on Wall Street. The Hermetica Fund really was a Ponzi scheme and so was Zunax. Hermetica had invested all its money in just three companies, one of which was Zunax. And Zunax, during the five-year reign of Milton Babst, had closed all its factories, terminated most of its employees and invested virtually all of its capital in Hermetica, resulting in earnings growth that pushed up Zunax's stock price at a phenomenal rate. This in turn accelerated Hermetica's rate of return, which fed Zunax's stock price, and so on, quarter after quarter, until the bubble burst. At the end we had fewer than three hundred employees, mostly bean counters counting non-existent beans as they tried to keep up with each other's emails. Evidently Bob Tedder had threatened to expose the truth, which explained his immunity from the rules that applied to everyone else. It remained for a sap like me, with no inkling of the truth, to be the company's most effective spokesman, using my skills as a fiction writer to craft a world of illusion that no one in his right mind—including myself—should have believed in.

At Hermetica all this had supposedly gone on without Gratzky's knowledge. When he realized what had happened he was already under indictment—thanks to the files supplied by Martin—and it was too late. The investigation had created its own fictional world and had to run its course, bringing about the catastrophe it was intended to avert. Now I was caught up in that investigation. My attorney has assured me that I have an excellent chance of avoiding jail time if I agree to cooperate. Apparently everyone else at Zunax is cooperating, including Bob Tedder, Julie Kim, and even Milton Babst. In fact so many people are cooperating that I can't imagine who's left to cooperate against. They say Bob Tedder is negotiating for a severance package.

Paul Gratzky himself has not had an easy time of it. Even before the indictment he was half crazed by the fear that his success had killed his closest friends and relatives, and when he learned about the Ponzi scheme it almost broke his heart. His supporters say if he'd discovered the fraud sooner he might have stopped it before it triggered a global market collapse. In any event, the demise of Hermetica pushed him over the edge. He now spends his time squatting on the floor of his hospital room with his legs crossed, endlessly chanting random lines from Billy Joel songs. I can only hope that Milton Babst, still snug in his Nepalese lamasery, will suffer a similar fate.

As for me, apart from my legal troubles I have the reproaches of an angry conscience to contend with. Six innocent people died because of me. How can I ever forgive myself for letting that happen? At first I tried to salve my conscience by blaming the whole thing on Jackie—she was the muse of violence, I told myself, who had inspired her husband's insane fury. But no, I soon admitted, Jackie wasn't to blame. Violence is inside us, as human as envy or anger or sex. Why else would we spend so much of our time reading about it, playing games with it, watching it on TV Some people inspire it, some carry it out; we all have our roles to play. Most of us sit by and watch it happen, knowing that if we're not content to be spectators we might be brought on stage. And then there are fools like me, who make a habit of disregarding the consequences of their actions. If anyone other than Falcone was to blame, that honor belonged to me. I went to bed with Jackie knowing she'd write a story about it, and all I cared about was whether she brought her story to the group. It never occurred to me to worry about how "Larry" might react, or what evils might be set in motion by what I did. So in reality I was more than the common thread that bound the victims together. I was the one who awakened the violence that led to their deaths.

Falcone has confessed to all the killings, including the man he mistakenly ran down in front of Brian's office thinking he was Brian. Falcone wasn't really a cop, of course. He was the owner of a small fleet of taxicabs based in the Bronx; his name wasn't even Falcone. That first time, when he came to my apartment in his cheap brown suit with his leering, suspicious eyes—when in fact his mission was to get everybody's name and address so he could track them down and kill them—we all thought he was a cop. He looked like a cop, he acted like a cop. He even had cards printed up that said he was a cop. But the second and third times I met him, when I was alone with him, the deception should have been obvious. Why didn't I see through it and call the police?

As I look back I realize Falcone was playing cat and mouse with me, daring me to thwart him. He made those midnight phone calls that could have been traced to his cell phone. He even left behind the Agatha Christie book I'd loaned to Jackie—*And Then There Were None*—and without Sara's deadly hands that's the way the story would have ended. For he was diabolically clever in planning and carrying out his crimes in exactly the right order. The police investigated each murder, but there was no apparent link between them. Jackie's death seemed to be a local street crime, and obviously Falcone didn't tell the police about the writers' group. Brian and Kate both lived by themselves and kept their writing a secret from everybody they knew. To anyone but the members of the group it wouldn't have been obvious that these deaths had anything to do with each other. Only when Eleanor died would the connection have been irresistible—at that point the game had to be played quickly to its conclusion. I cheated death, thanks to Sara. But my escape brought another humbling realization: the writers' group was so peripheral to the lives of its members that when they were murdered it didn't even find its way into the investigation.

I felt I owed Zelda an apology, having wrongly accused her of making the midnight phone calls. I had even been unfair to Wolfgang, who (I now realized) had every right to growl at me and give me the evil eye. The two of them must have sensed my change of heart. When I knocked on Zelda's door and identified myself, there was no growling or gnashing of teeth. Zelda greeted me politely and invited me in, even offered me a seat on her zebra-skin loveseat.

She looked haggard and depressed, her spiky hair drooping sadly, her eyes red and raw as if she'd been crying. You would never have known she was a mathematical genius or a Wall Street trader. All the genius had been knocked out of her, and all the spunk, leaving a pint-sized woman subdued by sorrow and pain. "I went to see Paul at the hospital," she said quietly, sitting across from me on a sling chair. "It was really creepy. A police ward for lunatics."

"Why did you go?"

"I thought I might be able to do him some good. He asked to see me."

I never really knew much about Zelda's relationship with Gratzky. It had ended before I met her—ended badly, I had surmised—and she never wanted to talk about it. Evidently his descent into madness had its beginnings in that earlier period as well.

"Paul didn't even know about the Ponzi scheme," she said. "The quants dreamed that up. They knew the fund's returns were dropping and they were desperate to keep the money coming in."

Wolfgang stood between Zelda and me, staring back at me like a ghost. I was tempted to pet him but thought better of it. "I've heard a theory that Gratzky's bad luck—all the seemingly random disasters that happened to him and his family—was somehow the result of his investment strategy."

Zelda seemed taken aback, as if I'd uncovered one of her darkest secrets. "That's what drove him crazy," she muttered, avoiding my eyes. "He began by arbitraging risk and ended up trying to squeeze every last bit of random variation out of every market in the world."

This was starting to sound a little too much like one of Josh's science fiction stories. "Go on," I said warily.

"Paul was locked in a battle with randomness, with chance. To the extent he succeeded in eliminating chance from the universe, he changed it into a deterministic one. He was playing God."

"Playing God?"

"That's why he went nuts," she nodded. "He gave away enormous sums of money to fund research on the diseases and freak accidents that killed his family because he desperately wanted to know if they were the result of blind chance or had some deeper cause. And as time went on he came to believe that he had caused them himself. He came to believe that he had brought about all the evils of the world. No, not just evils—Evil itself."

"But how?"

"By using the randomness of the universe for his own purposes."

I looked up and realized that she had tears in her eyes. "When I was working at Hermetica, Paul fell in love with me," she said. "If you can believe that."

"And then?"

"And then…" Her voice trailed off. "Since he was sure that loving me would have the same effect it had on his wife and his kids and everybody else he ever loved, he fired me from Hermetica and refused to ever see me again. He called it a sacrifice."

I touched her hand. "Josh called it the revenge of the improbable," I said.

"Yes," she nodded. "That's what I would call it too."

Back in my apartment, I wondered if something similar might have happened to our writers' group. Each of us, as a storyteller, tried to control every detail of the little world we created. That's what you do when you write fiction, you try to find the truth by shaping a perfect falsehood, an invented universe without anomalies or chance deviations. Of course we were doomed to failure. We were all unreliable narrators, just like Paul Gratzky and Bob Tedder and the Wall Street pundits and the TV meteorologists. The more we succeeded in imposing our own visions on the world, the less that world resembled the real one. The harder we struggled against chance and incoherence, the more random and unrealistic our writing became. Jackie exposed the first loose threads, holding them up to be unraveled, one story at a time, by Eleanor and then Brian, Kate, Sara and Josh, each entangling the others in a new web of delusion and distrust. And I did my part, like a diabolical stage director, explaining and interpreting and urging them on until we had tallied more dead bodies than the last scene of *Hamlet*. Yes, the story began when the conflict began, but we were so caught up in our petty elaborations that the real conflict and the real evil were invisible until it was too late. Any critic would have derided this ludicrous chain of events as utterly beyond the pale. Could anything have been more improbable?

Yet sometimes the revenge of the improbable works the other way. Dr. G put it this way, when I told him I could no longer afford our Sunday morning chess games: "Just when you're being swept out to sea by a hurricane, you catch a stiff breeze in your bandanna and it floats you up to New York City, where there's enough fools aching to lose their money to keep a doctor busy the rest of his life." In other words, sometimes the revenge of the improbable works in your favor and then we call it serendipity. Against all the odds you end up with something truer and finer than you could have imagined even in your insular little world. In my case that something was Sara.

I had some legal issues to face but I was confident that with the help of my high-priced attorney I would come out in one piece. To keep body and soul together, I took a job at the Starbucks on Fifth Avenue not far from Sara's office. In spite of all that had happened I wasn't ready to give up on my writing and I wasn't ready to give up on Sara. Now that I was done spinning out mendacious press releases maybe I could actually write something worth reading. It was my work at Zunax, I realized, that had brought on my writer's block. Now I felt as if a crushing weight had been lifted from my soul. The words started seeping out a few at a time, then the flow increased until whole sentences, paragraphs and chapters were pouring into my laptop three or four hours every night. This change didn't surprise me. How can you spend the day telling lies and then search for the truth in your spare time? I'd learned some hard lessons and I suspected there were harder ones in the curriculum. But life would go on, and I meant to be there when it did.

As the only survivors of the writers' group, Sara and I had a moral obligation to continue its work. At least that's what I told her as we shared a cup of coffee one afternoon at Starbucks during my break. It was another rainy afternoon, which was all we seemed to have anymore. I'd read over some of her early stories, the ones she'd brought me before she joined the group. They were as sharp as etched marble, deeply human, though her main character—invariably a dark-haired woman about her age—viewed the world from an ironic distance of astronomical proportions. She was always a rich man's daughter, the graduate of an Ivy League school, usually an artist in conflict with her ambitious mother. Sara's reality, as I'd learned, could not have been more different. Were her stories the equivalent of my Zunax press releases? Or were they her way of discovering herself outside the limitations of her life? Beneath the deceptions I could discern a caring but troubled soul, a keen intellect, a true heart. I wanted to give her—and myself—the benefit of the doubt. I wanted to believe that both Sara and I could be the strong, complex characters we imagined in our stories, not the unreliable narrators we'd shown ourselves to be in real life.

As we sat sipping our coffee, she filled me in on her activities since the confrontation with Falcone. She was depressed, rattled by the experience of paralyzing Falcone and almost being killed herself. Her minimalism had been challenged and proved inadequate to real life. As if that wasn't enough, her mother had passed away a few days before. I wanted her to know that I was there for her, but I felt embarrassed by my own past deceptions. I tried to explain why I continued with the writers' group after I'd stopped writing myself. It was probably because I knew at some level that my work for Zunax was fraudulent. If I couldn't write, at least I could help other people realize their dreams. And now—though I didn't say this—I wanted to help Sara realize her dreams, with me in them. And I wanted her to help me realize mine.

"Would you like to have dinner this Saturday night?" I asked her.

She smiled warily. "Frankly, I don't want to go out with anybody right now. I need some time to myself. I'm still pretty upset about everything that's happened."

"I understand."

She drank the last of her coffee. "I'm glad you don't seem to mind that I misled you—well, let's face it, lied to you—about who I am."

"I'm as guilty of that as you are."

"Well, it bothers me even if it doesn't bother you." She stood up to leave, clearing her trash off the table. "I'd better get back to the office."

I followed her out the door, even though my break was technically over. Outside on Fifth Avenue it was raining cats and dogs and Sara had the only umbrella, but a tsunami wouldn't have kept me from walking along beside her. Somehow I felt emboldened by the thundering downpour and the fact that we had to huddle together under the umbrella.

"Sara," I hollered, "I don't care about your little flaws or even the big flaws you think you have. I know who you are even if you don't. I haven't been misled or deceived about you for one minute."

"I don't believe you, Will," she yelled, plunging ahead without looking at me.

"If you give me a chance I can help you live up to those stories you wrote about yourself and even surpass them."

Her laughter clattered over the rain. "Is that the highest achievement you can imagine?" she shouted, slipping her arm around my elbow. "To be as real as a work of fiction?"

"Not as real," I said, "but as true."

"As true?" She stopped and turned to face me, smiling back at me in wonderment. The rainwater washed over our feet as if we were standing in a mountain stream. "What do you mean?"

"Being true," I said. "Isn't that what fiction is all about?"

Sara's Journal
August 16

Time to get this journal going again. Mom accepted my forgiveness (I like to think) with her eyes before she died. So I ought to be able to forgive myself too. Dad's been a big help; even Freddie seems smarter than he used to be. Among other vanities, I've given up pretending to be what I'm not.

I like Will, but he's definitely a fixer-upper; he needs work. He's going to have to find a new hobby, maybe mountain climbing or bungee jumping or deep-sea diving—anyway something a lot less dangerous than writing fiction. He'll always be high maintenance, a dreamer who needs a muse just to get through the day. He seems a little deluded about me. Maybe that's a good thing—maybe I ought to listen to him instead of my own nagging doubts. He keeps asking me out and I keep turning him down, just like Mario Migliori. Next time— just to see what happens— I think I'll say yes.

THE END

Author's Note and Acknowledgements

Bruce Hartman lives with his wife in Philadelphia. He has worked as a pianist, music teacher, bookseller and attorney and has been writing fiction for many years. His most recent book, *The Rules of Dreaming*, was published by Swallow Tail Press in May 2013. *Kirkus Reviews*, in awarding it the Kirkus Star for Books of Exceptional Merit, called it "a mind-bending marriage of ambitious literary theory and classic murder mystery." His first novel, *Perfectly Healthy Man Drops Dead*, won the Salvo Press Mystery Novel Award and was published by Salvo Press in 2008. You can read more on his website, www.brucehartmanbooks.

Special thanks to Martha, Jack, Tom, Kelly and Isabel for their invaluable support on this project.

Made in the USA
Lexington, KY
10 November 2013